SING INTO YOUR
STORM

TIMOTHY D. JOHNSON

©2015 Timothy D. Johnson
Printed by BT Johnson Publishing
www.BTJohnsonPublishing.com
Toll Free: 1-866-260-9563

Printed in the United States of America
ISBN: 978-1-938311-18-5

DEDICATION

My deepest love and appreciation to my Lord and Savior, Jesus Christ, whose relentless pursuit, finally apprehended me. He put a song in my heart… An eternal Love Song… It is a song that we will sing *together* forever… A song that will be sung as a Duet…*The Song of the Lamb*…

And to my precious wife Betty, whose love, encouragement, sacrifice, patience and laughter has been the most profound gift to me. I cherish you! Your worth is far above rubies…

THE TABLE OF TREASURES

THE HEAVEN SONG

"THE SOUND OF MANY WATERS..."

The Scriptures provide us a preponderance of evidence that long before the world began, the beauty of *song* existed in Heaven and was used to exalt the Lord our God. We see it in the glorious processions of worship all around His Throne.

Scripture teaches even *before* the foundations of the world were laid, (which we shall call eternity past) Lucifer (now called Satan) was the Chief <u>musician</u> of Heaven– leading unending and ecstatic praise & worship unto Him that sits on the Throne.. Lucifer himself, was actually created at some point *with* tambourines and flutes adorning him – long before our world was ever created!

"…The workmanship of your timbrels and pipes
was prepared for you on the day you were created."
(Ezekiel 28:13)

Even at the very dawn of creation itself - the Scriptures say:

"the morning stars (angels) *sang* together,
and all the sons of God *shouted* for joy!"
(Job 38:7)

And at the fall of Lucifer from Heaven… the Bible tells us:

"Your pomp is brought down to Sheol, with the
sound of your *stringed instruments*… (i.e. harps)
(Isaiah 14:11)

Through this glimpses into eternity past it is pretty *clear* that Heaven Song continually filled the atmosphere of the Throne of God – and it *always* will…

One the most amazing insights into worship and *song* before this same Throne of God, is from of the Book of Revelation. St. John the Divine was lifted up into Heaven through an extraordinary revelatory experience and was later allowed to write about the things he saw… And what did John see? He says that he saw a "Lamb…"

Certainly there were many, many things in Heaven that *might* have caught John's attention, but the thing he was most transfixed upon on was The <u>Lamb</u> in the center of the Throne.

"Then I looked, and behold, a <u>Lamb</u> standing on
Mount Zion, and with Him, one hundred and
forty-four thousand, having His Father's name
written on their foreheads. And I heard a *voice*
from Heaven, like the *sound* of many waters…
and like the *voice* of loud thunder. And I heard the
sound of harpists playing their harps. They *sang* as
it were a *new song* before the Throne…"
(Revelation 14:2)

The *sound* of many waters…. This gives us a beautiful picture of deep, intimate worship before the Throne of God. The very word *sound* translates - the *tone* from *musical instruments* coupled with *speech, language, utterances* (*song*) coming from a thunderous multitude that is numerous in attendance i.e. representing many streams (*waters*) flowing *together* to form a *river* of praise! The sound of many waters!

Transparent worshippers, pure, holy, in perfect harmony, burning in zeal and passion for The _Lamb_ of God. John described it this way:

"And I saw what looked like a sea of glass,
mingled with fire…"
(Revelation 15:2)

Again we see the imagery John is describing as a pure, crystal like, flowing river:

"And he showed me a pure river of water
of life, clear as crystal, proceeding from
the Throne of God _and_ of The _Lamb_…
(Revelation 22:1)

This is the Throne of Almighty God and of The _Lamb_ who "seemed to have been slain". This very place is also _your_ Eternal home…

"For _you_ have come to Mount Zion, and to
the city of the living God, the _heavenly_ Jerusalem,
to an innumerable company of angels, to the general
assembly and church of the Firstborn… _whose names_
are **registered** in Heaven, and to God, the Judge of all,
to the spirits of just men made perfect, to Jesus the
Mediator of the New Covenant, and to the Blood of
sprinkling that speaks better things than _that of_ Abel.
(Hebrews 12:22-24)

Yes, _you_ have been _registered_ in that very place, for the Word of God declares:

"The LORD loves the gates of Zion, more than all the
dwellings of Jacob! Glorious things are spoken
of you, O city of God! _Selah_. This _one_ was born there…

And of Zion it will be said, this *one* and that *one* were **born** in her; and the Most High Himself shall establish her. The LORD will **record**, when He **registers** the peoples: This *one* was born <u>there</u>. *Selah.* Both the *singers* and the players on instruments say *(sing)* all my springs (fountains) are in You."
(Psalms 87:2-7)

When did this happen? The *Lamb's* Book of Life (in which <u>*your*</u> name is **recorded**) was:

"*Written* before the foundation of the world…
of The <u>*Lamb*</u> who has been slain."
(Revelation 13:8)

Not only were you *recorded* in the Lamb's Book of Life before the foundation of the world, but the Lord also *registered* you even into Himself!

"See, I have inscribed (engraved) <u>*you*</u> on the palms of My hands; <u>*your*</u> walls are continually before Me."
(Isaiah 49:16)

You might ask is this really speaking of <u>*me*</u>? Does this really refer to <u>*me*</u> personally? The Word of God teaches us that:

"**If <u>*you*</u>** were "Buried with Him (in baptism)…
<u>*you*</u> were *also* **raised** with Him through faith in the working of God."
(Colossians 2:12),

"And God **raised** us up with Christ and <u>*seated us with Him*</u> in the heavenly places

in Christ Jesus…"
(Ephesians 2:6)

In both instances the word "*raised*" is past tense, meaning that the act has already happened…You were created for worship!

You have a *rightful* and *purposeful* place right <u>now</u> before the Throne of God. Not as a spectator (there are no spectators in Heaven), but rather as the Redeemed of the Lord!! There is an order of worship you have been called to join and you have been seated before the Throne of God for. Join the Royal Procession! <u>You</u> have a *worshipful* and *priestly* order to fulfill!

For <u>you</u> are "A *chosen* generation, a *Royal* priesthood,
a holy nation, <u>His own special people</u>, that <u>you</u> may
proclaim the **praises** of Him who called <u>you</u> out of
darkness, into <u>His</u> marvelous light."
(1 Peter 2:0)

"Let the redeemed of the Lord say so!"
(Psalms 107:20)

Yes, you, the Redeemed, have been called to declare His praises in *song*… Forever you will be *singing* – the Heaven Song!!

There are processions of living worship that goes before the Throne of God and before The <u>*Lamb*</u> - continually… <u>You</u> were created by design for the praise & worship of the Lord <u>*your*</u> God, and <u>*your*</u> King! <u>You</u> play a significant role in the worship protocols of the Throne Room of God as a *participant* in those Holy processions! Imagine joining in of the casting of crowns, the falling down prostrate before His awesomeness Glory in awe and wonder! Ministering unto Him unending. Gazing and beholding His beauty… Joining with Jesus in fervent Intercession unto The Father. What a glorious picture of some of the roles in Heaven _you_ have been called to! _You_ were created to join the Heaven Song!

All around the Throne, in this glorious and majestic praise, a company of innumerable angels of all different kinds and ranks, never stop worshipping Him who sits on The Throne… The Seraphim angels, (thought to rank as the highest in angelic order because of their Divine Love & Zeal), reportedly even outrank the covering Cherubim angels! Can _you_ envision being surrounded by the great cloud of witnesses, (the Saints of all time), the 24 Elders, and the Four Living Creatures, completely engulfed into a harmonious symphony of ecstatic praise and worship unto The Living God! But even this is not _all_ that happens in Heaven…

For even the Lord God Himself moves powerfully in The Heaven Song! Zephaniah saw this in his day and recorded it! Yes, the Lord _sings_! The Lord rejoices over _you_!

"For the LORD your God is in _your_ midst,
the Mighty One, will save; He will rejoice
over _you_ with gladness, He will quiet _you_ with
His Love, He will rejoice over _you_ with _singing_."
(Zephaniah 3:17)

The book of Hebrews tells us that God is _unchanging_, as He _always was_, He still is today and _will be_ forever more:

"Jesus Christ *is* the same yesterday,
today, and *forever*."
(Hebrews 13:8)

He has always been… He always is… and He will always be…
John gives us important revelation and insight into this
Eternal God from the very beginning of the Gospel of John:

"In the beginning was The Word, and The Word
was _with_ God, and The Word _was_ God. He was in
the beginning with God. All things were made
through Him, and without Him *nothing* was made
that was made. In Him was life, and the life was
the light of men."
(John 1:1-4)

Now we know from Scripture that Heaven Song existed and
flowed, long before the dawn of creation… Right? We see in
Scripture the worshipping Angels and musical instruments at
work long before the foundation of the earth had ever been
laid.

We know that the Lord Himself, *never* changes… He is the
same yesterday, today and forever… Right?

"For I am the LORD, I change not."
(Malachi 3:6)

We also know that the Lord *sings* over us too… Right?

Question: Just how long do you think the Lord has been
singing over us? Just since the days of Zephaniah when
Zephaniah recorded his writings? Could the Lord have been

singing over us much further back? Would it be a reach to imagine the Lord singing over us and about us - all the way from eternity past? Perhaps the weight of Scripture can help:

"…Just as He ***chose*** us in Him
before the foundation of the world,
that we should be holy and without
blame before Him in love."
(Ephesians 1:4)

"…And that He might make known the riches
of His glory on the vessels of mercy, which
He had prepared ***before-hand*** for glory."
(Romans 9:23)

"For whom He ***foreknew***, He also pre-destined to
be conformed to the image of His Son…"
(Romans 8:29)

Let's take an even closer look at this… There are two amazing glimpses in Scripture that allow us to *see* the eternal, intentionality of God, and His *heavenly* orchestration… that is, the plans and purposes that the Lord was *developing* in both His mind and His heart from ***before*** time as we know it (i.e. before the creation of this world). Again for point of reference, we will simply refer to this as eternity past… from ***before*** the foundation of the earth…

In Psalms 139, the sweet psalmist of Israel, King David, recorded a profound revelatory insight into this *intentionality* of the God of Heaven concerning his life – ***before*** time ever began…and we know this revelation came directly from the

Holy Spirit since "<u>All Scripture</u> is given by *inspiration* of God (that is…God breathed)." (2 Timothy 3:16)

David declared in Psalm 139 that:
- A. That God ***knew*** everything about David (vs. 1-4)
- B. That God ***created*** every part of him (vs. 13, 14)
- C. That God ***recorded*** the secrets of David's creation ***<u>before</u>*** he was ever born - in His Book (vs. 13-16)
- D. That God had ***fashioned*** David's days (determined them) – ***<u>before</u>*** there ever was one… (vs. 16)
- E. That God's *thoughts* ***<u>from</u>*** eternity <u>*about*</u> David outnumbered the sands of the seashore (vs. 17-18)

In Jeremiah Chapter 1, the Lord makes an extraordinary comment to the young prophet:
- A. "***<u>Before</u>*** I formed you in the womb, I ***<u>knew</u>*** you; ***<u>Before</u>*** you were <u>*born*</u> I <u>*sanctified*</u> you; I <u>*ordained*</u> you a prophet to the nations."

It would do us well to more definitively understand the *choice* of words the Lord used in communicating to Jeremiah, and the eternal *considerations* and *plans* that God had made concerning Jeremiah, ***<u>before</u>*** he was ever born. It would help us to understand as well, that like Jeremiah and David, <u>*we*</u> too are not just an *afterthought* in the mind and heart of God from eternity past…. Here is more insight into those words and their meaning:

1. ***<u>Before</u>***: indicates before birth or one's coming forth
2. ***<u>Knew</u>***: have knowledge of, acquainted with <u>*before*</u>
3. ***<u>Sanctified</u>***: declared as holy, consecrated, set apart
4. ***<u>Ordained</u>***: make, form, constitute towards a destiny

So here the Lord has chosen to reveal how well *acquainted* and *purposeful* He is in the lives of His people - from eternity past… As the Lord spoke to Israel (as they were entering captivity in Babylon), even then, He reveals His heart for them – not on the spur of the moment, but well *considered*, *deliberate* and *intentional* towards their well-being (even in judgement…)

"For I **know** the **thoughts** (meditates, purposes,
plots) that I **think** towards you, says the LORD,
thoughts of peace and not of evil, to give you
a *future* and a *hope*."
(Jeremiah 29:11)

We know this to be true because Jeremiah was prophesying about God's *intentions* to Israel beyond the 70 years captivity that they were just about to enter…

Our God is *intentional* concerning **us** too! He has spent much of eternity past *contemplating* and *planning, ordaining* and *fashioning* the lives of His people. The Bible says it's He who: "**Knows** and **declares** the end from the *beginning*, and **from ancient times** *things* that are not *yet* done, saying, My counsel shall stand, and I will do *all* of My good pleasure."
(Isaiah 46:10)

"A man's steps are *ordered* (ordained)
of the Lord."
(Proverbs 20:24)

God has a *plan* for *you* fashioned from eternity…

****

Author's Note: Although the writer of this book has been zealously committed to honor the tenants of the Word of God, with special regard to:

"Not going beyond what is written"
(1 Corinthians 4:6).

The rest of this chapter has been written from the standpoint of supposition (suppose that…or what if? etc.) The motivation of such discourse is to stir the reader to ponder (but not wander) and to meditate upon the Word of God. The author intently believes the concluding substance of this chapter that he shares – but _challenges_ each reader to be Berean in spirit, and to diligently search out the Scriptures for yourself to see if these things be true… and to experience what witness of the Spirit the Lord may give _you_ in these matters.

The school of thought discussed below, must have its final rendering determined by each reader _individually_… This text is written primarily in the form of a question… to provoke thought and meditation on the Scriptures. The author would highly recommend reading (or re-reading) "Destined for the Throne" by Paul Billheimer as an excellent supporting book reference (Paul's book is endorsed by Billy Graham).

If God has _pondered your_ precious life over and over, as the very _betrothed_ of The _Lamb_, that is, the very one _destined_ to become the _Spouse_ of God… Would you not think from the echelons of eternity past that the Lord has _delighted_ over you countless times, and that He has _rejoiced_ over _you_, the very one who will eventually become His Bride, since the eternal purpose of the Lord is His Church?

And since we know from the Book of Zephaniah that the Lord *rejoices* over you and *sings* over you – could His *song* have been *sang* over you from eternity (past) in the midst of His *thoughts, intentions* and *plans* for you - which Scripture tells us are indeed from **before** the foundation of the earth?

Could His *song* have even been a prophetic declaration of what was to come for His Bride to be, concerning His Love and His plans for her destiny sang from eternity past unto eventual prophetic fulfillment? Are not His thoughts (plans) for *you* are as numerous as the sands of the seashore?

So **if** this were true, that the Lord has *sang* over you from eternity (past) (and not just from the actual days of Zephaniah's vision), would *you* not *wonder* just what God might be *singing* about *you*, seeing how *intentional* He is?
Could it be that Jesus is *singing* an eternal *Love Song* both about *you* and to *you*, His future Bride? **If** that were so, what an amazing *song* that must be....

Another thought... Throughout the book of Revelation, St. John the Divine continually sees Jesus as "The *Lamb* who sits on the Throne." Though he *hears* a Lion, he *sees* a *Lamb*.... How long do you think there has been imagery of Jesus as The *Lamb* sitting on the Throne? Wasn't the Book of Life written **before** the foundation of the earth? And this Book was not just "A Book of Life" *because* it was referred to as The *Lamb's* Book of Life... *written* **before** the foundation of the earth." Would this not suggest the imagery of The *Lamb* from eternity past?

Does this lend weight to the notion that perhaps Jesus was in the likeness of The _**Lamb**_ who sits on the Throne – long _**before**_ time began? Does not the Word of God say that "The _**Lamb**_ of God was slain _from_ (_**before**_) the foundation of the world?

The first thing John the Baptist declares, upon seeing Jesus _as_ the living God was:
"Behold the _**Lamb**_ of God, who taketh away
the sins of the world."
(Johns 1:29)

Was Jesus was The _**Lamb**_ before Calvary? The _**Lamb**_ _**before**_ time? Is Jesus Christ not The Eternal _**Lamb**_ of God?

So again, **if** in fact it has been The _"**Lamb"**_ who has been _singing_ over you, what might The _**Lamb**_ of God be _singing_? Could it be _The Song of The **Lamb**_ that Jesus has singing over _you_ from eternity past?

If the Song of Moses was taught, written and _sung_ by Moses, could _The Song of the **Lamb**_ have been written and _sung_ by The _**Lamb**_ Himself?

Could that _song_ actually be a duet, having interactive _participation_ from both the initiator/author (Christ Jesus) and from His _intended_ recipient - as an eternal Love _song_ for the Bridegroom and the Bride to _sing_ over each other?

Could The Bridegroom have left open stanzas for The Bride to join in _singing_ portions of this _song_ back to The _Lamb_ spontaneously as a Love response to His affirmations of the eternal Love that He has been _singing_ over her?

Doesn't the Bible say there will be victorious ones in Heaven who will *sing*:

"The *song* of Moses <u>and</u>
the *song* of The <u>*Lamb*</u>?
(Revelation 15:3)

Could one song be about a mighty deliverance(s), and the other about the greatest Love Story ever told - concerning a wedding to take place in eternity, that was crafted ***<u>before</u>*** time ever began?

Even more fantastic, could *the Song <u>of</u> the* <u>**Lamb**</u> be so revelatory and creative, coming from an *omniscient* (all knowing), and *omnipotent* (all powerful) God that the Bride (the soon to be Wife of The <u>**Lamb**</u>) herself, could have actually have been inaugurated or born right out of the heart and mind of The <u>**Lamb**</u> as he sang His *Song* across eternity… *The Song <u>of</u> the* <u>**Lamb**</u>?

Could you imagine such an incredible *<u>plan</u>,* for The <u>***Lamb's***</u> Wife to be joined to Him for eternity, as a co-regent Bride to sit with Him on His Throne, a Bride who would lay down her life for Him (after Him having <u>first</u> laid down His life for her) – and both of them doing it voluntarily because of Love?

If this were true, wouldn't it become the Love Story of Eternity? Can you imagine a Bride, actually made in God's image, literally becoming the *next of kin* to the Lord God, forever destined to be The <u>***Lamb's***</u> Wife *forever*? Would this not be Glorious?

"For the Glory of a Man is His Wife."
(1 Corinthians 11:7)

It is believed that Lucifer had among the deepest and closest relationship to our God, who sits the Throne, of any *created* being *ever*, and that he was the *covering* Cherub over this very Throne. As the Chief *musician* of Heaven, he continuously lead an innumerable company of other angels into unending, ecstatic and gloriously crescendo's of worship unto the Almighty God for a time span beyond our comprehension, who knows - perhaps trillions and trillions of man years just to try and gain concept of eternity past…

But somewhere along the courses of Heaven, the news of The **_Lamb's_** intention to create a Wife for Himself to sit *with* Him on His Throne *forever* was announced… Again, could it have come through a spontaneous prophetic *song* The **_Lamb_** *sang* into existence?

Enraptured in the Shekinah Glory of God's Presence & Beauty incessantly, how might this news have affected Lucifer? We know from Scripture that something came between Lucifer and the God who sits on the Throne…Could the news that The **_Lamb_** was going to create a Wife with far more privilege and relationship to God than Lucifer enjoyed for so long be the very thing that interrupted his continuous worship of God for so long?

Could this event have been the turning point that created envy? Could jealousy have played a role in Lucifer wanting to be like the Most High and wanting to ascend himself? Could this revelation have spurned his hatred towards God's creation, and his ultimate determination to spend all his time and energy trying to hurt and separate creation from the very Marriage Supper of The **_Lamb_** after he was cast out of Heaven?

∎∎∎

The Heaven Song is a very special gift the Lord has given to <u>us</u>. It can be deeply worshipful unto The **_Lamb_**, it can be prophetic, declarative, powerful, glorious, and eternal. Through the course of this book, <u>*you*</u> will see from Scripture how this precious gift of God can be used as a mighty weapon in the midst of the storms that come into <u>*your*</u> life. Through *The Heaven Song* <u>*you*</u> can overcome all adversity – and simultaneously give God the highest worship that He is so worthy of – for through *The Heaven Song* you can pass through your Red Sea with praise – right <u>*through*</u> the impassible way!!

JOIN THE HEAVEN SONG!!

THE SONG OF MIRIAM

"RIGHT SONG – WRONG SIDE"

he Great Deliverance of the Children of Israel out of Egypt (the House of Bondage) stands as one the Bible's most incredible displays of God's Mighty Hand.

For over 400 years, the offspring of Abraham were mercilessly oppressed under slavery by the weight of heavy taskmasters. There was a burdening "cry" from the slaves that reached the ears (Heart) of God, a cry of despair from the deepest place of anguish and torment a soul could ever know…

"And the Lord said: I have surely *seen* the
oppression (affliction) of My people who
are in Egypt, and have *heard* their *cry* because
of their taskmasters, for I *know* their sorrows".
(Exodus 3:7)

Can you imagine being born into the House of Bondage during that time? From the moment your eyes see the light of day at birth, until the moment your eyes are closed in death, the entirety of your life you would only know pain, suffering and toil. An entire life lived in captivity, never knowing the joy of even one day of freedom.

The torture of this imprisonment continued from generation to generation – where hope was a distant thing of the past. Why was God not answering them in their great distress? Where was the Covenant that Yahweh cut with Abraham and his descendants? Had not the Lord himself *promised* that He would bless Abraham's descendants, and give them the land of Canaan? How could they believe this in the land of sorrows?

But the Lord God did have a plan:

"Because the LORD loves you, and because
He would *keep* the oath which He *swore* to
your fathers, the LORD has brought you out
with a mighty hand, and redeemed you from
the house of bondage, from the hand of Pharaoh,
King of Egypt.

Therefore *know* that the LORD your God, He is God,
the *faithful* God who <u>keeps</u> covenant and mercy for a
thousand generations with those who love Him and
<u>keep</u> His commandments."
(Deuteronomy 7:8-9)

And lead them out He did…

"Remember this day, in which you went out of Egypt,
out of the house of bondage; for by the *strength of hand*
the Lord brought you out of this place."
(Exodus 13:3)

But in the *plan* of God, He did not lead them in the *expected path* and neither will He lead you in an *expected path*. The most likely route for their journey to Canaan was by way of the Philistines, for it was the nearest, most convenient course. But again, God had a much more specific *plan* He was orchestrating…

"So the children of Israel went *around* by way
of the wilderness of the Red Sea. Even so, they
marched in orderly ranks."
(Exodus 13:17)

This meant they were organized in fighting formation. But they had the Shekinah Presence of God going before them day and night – cloud by day, fire by night!

The Lord *intentionally* led them to camp by the sea. They were at the height of faith and confidence! The Word of God says:

"The children of Israel went out in **boldness**."
(Exodus 14:8)

But the Lord had hardened the heart of Pharaoh, so much so that he regretted letting the Israelites go, and he sent _all_ of his horses, chariots and armies to pursuit them!

The armies of Pharaoh surrounded them at their encampment by the sea. The stage was set... There was nowhere to go... The impassible sea was in front of them and the angry Egyptian army encircled all around the other way... They had three choices… Surrender, fight or trust God.

But the children of Israel *chose* to trust their *eyes* and not their God... Suddenly now gripped with great fear and panic (what happened to the **boldness**), they forgot about the great deliverance the Lord had _just_ brought them out with - by His Mighty Hand, and the mighty miracles of the 10 plagues God brought upon Egypt… They forgot about carrying out the wealth of Egypt, and being led forth out of Egypt by the Glory Presence of God – a cloud by day, fire by night!

In an instant, there was a massive *change* of heart. Consumed with fear, they:

"…Cried out unto the Lord."
(Exodus 14:10).

But their cry was not a heart cry of faith or *expectancy* in their God. Blinded from even the *thought* of breakthrough, they turned on Moses with insolence and contemptuous rage:

"Because there were no graves in Egypt,
have *you* taken us away to die in the
wilderness? Why have *you* so dealt with
us, to bring us out of Egypt?"

For it would have been better for us to
serve the Egyptians than that we should
die in the wilderness."
(Exodus 14:11-12)

And Moses said to the people (actually prophesying to them):

"Do *not* be afraid. Stand still and see the
Salvation of the Lord, which He will
accomplish for you today. For the Egyptians
whom you see today, you shall see again no
more forever. The Lord will fight for you,
and you shall hold your peace."
(Exodus 14:13-14)

This is the very point, place and time where God revealed His intention in bringing them to this *place of encounter*. Remember it was God that had *intentionally* led them towards to this specific place, instead of taking the main (convenient) road through Philistia towards Canaan. It was also the Lord who had hardened Pharaoh's heart, causing him to relent about freeing the children of Israel and then deciding to go back after them again. God *set this stage* – at the Sea of Reeds called "yam suph" in Hebrew (later referred to as the Red Sea).

And the Lord spoke to Moses,

"Why do you cry to Me? Tell the children
of Israel to **_go forward_**!"
(Exodus 14:15).

Forward meant marching *directly* towards the water! So that
was the *plan* God had for the children of Israel – all along?

He was the one who led them to this very place, and He was
the one who had hardened Pharaoh's heart so that he would
come after Israelites.

Now the Lord had every intention of delivering His people...
But He wanted them to *learn* His ways - by taking a step of
faith *first*, in the midst of their first storm outside of Egypt.
God was also about to demonstrate to the most powerful ruler
and army upon the face of the earth, the raw *Power, Glory and
Faithfulness* of the God of Israel!

So Moses prophesied to them that the Lord was about to
deliver them:

 "Stand still and see the Salvation of the Lord
the He will accomplish for you _today_…The Lord
will fight for you, and you shall see His peace."
(Exodus 14: 13-14)

In the same way, _your_ God has every intention of delivering
you through your storm(s) too! He longs for you to *set* your
eyes on Him and take your first steps *forward* to walk right in
and through the impassible way! *Sing* into _your_ Red Sea!!

"For many are the afflictions of the righteous,
but the LORD *delivers* them out of them _all_."
(Psalms 34:19)

Then suddenly the Cloud Presence of God appeared,
descending right down unto the backs of the children of

Israel, separating them from the Egyptian armies. As night fell, that Presence became a pillar of fire keeping the Egyptians back from attacking them all night. It was literally a firewall of God's Shekinah Glory protecting them!

Let God's Glory come and surround _you_ in the midst, as _you_ are encountering your raging storm(s)!

"The Glory of God may be _your_ rear guard."
(Isaiah 58:8)

"For I, declares the LORD, will be a wall of fire
around her, and I will be the Glory in her midst."
(Zechariah 2:5)

As Moses stretched his hand out over the sea, it divided into a wall of water on both the left and the right. The children of Israel passed through – on dry ground!

Eventually the Egyptian army were able to pursue, and when they were fully inside the midst of the sea passage, the waters suddenly came swiftly down. Not even one from the Egyptian army survived!

When they reached the other side, _then_ they began to sing victoriously. They sang _The Song of Moses_ and _The Song of Miriam_. These were songs of triumph in the Lord!

The Song of Moses

Then Moses and the children of Israel sang this song to
the LORD, and spoke, saying:

"I will _sing_ to the LORD,
For He has triumphed gloriously!
The horse and its rider
He has thrown into the sea!

The LORD *is* my strength and song,
And He has become my salvation;
He is my God, and I will praise Him;
My father's God, and I will exalt Him.
The LORD is a man of war;
The LORD is His name.
Pharaoh's chariots and his army He has cast into the sea;
His chosen captains also are drowned in the Red Sea.
The depths have covered them;
They sank to the bottom like a stone.

Your right hand, O LORD, has become glorious in power;
Your right hand, O LORD, has dashed the enemy in pieces.
And in the greatness of Your excellence
You have overthrown those who rose against You;
You sent forth Your wrath;
It consumed them like stubble.
And with the blast of Your nostrils
The waters were gathered together;
The floods stood upright like a heap;
The depths congealed in the heart of the sea.
The enemy said, I will pursue,
I will overtake,
I will divide the spoil;
My desire shall be satisfied on them.
I will draw my sword,
My hand shall destroy them.
You blew with Your wind,
The sea covered them;
They sank like lead in the mighty waters.

Who *is* like You, O LORD, among the gods?
Who *is* like You, glorious in holiness,
Fearful in praises, doing wonders?

You stretched out Your right hand;
The earth swallowed them.
You in Your mercy have led forth
The people whom You have redeemed;
You have guided them in Your strength
To Your holy habitation.

"The people will hear and be afraid;
Sorrow will take hold of the inhabitants of Philistia.
Then the chiefs of Edom will be dismayed;
The mighty men of Moab,
Trembling will take hold of them;
All the inhabitants of Canaan will melt away.
Fear and dread will fall on them;
By the greatness of Your arm
They will be as still as a stone,
Till Your people pass over, O LORD,
Till the people pass over
Whom You have purchased.
You will bring them in and plant them
In the mountain of Your inheritance,
In the place, O LORD, which You have made
For Your own dwelling,
The sanctuary, O Lord, which Your
hands have established.
The LORD shall reign forever and ever."
(Exodus 15:1-18)

The Song of Miriam

Then Miriam the prophetess, the sister of Aaron,
took the timbrel in her hand; and all the women
went out after her with timbrels and with dances.
And Miriam answered them:

"Sing to the LORD,
For He has triumphed gloriously!
The horse and its rider
He has thrown into the sea!"
(Exodus 15:20-21)

What an incredible picture of triumphant praise, the children of Israel celebrating the great and mighty deliverance from the hands of Pharaoh and his armies! All in such dramatic and glorious splendor!

Yet within three days of this unprecedented exaltation of their God, these same cheerful, jubilant people turned from awesome rejoicing to great murmuring at the waters of Marah which were bitter.

"Now when they came to Marah, they could
not drink the waters of Marah, for they were
bitter. Therefore the name of it was called
Marah. And the people complained against
Moses, saying, what shall we drink?"
(Exodus 15: 23-24)

Now they were only perhaps seventy two hours removed from what had been one of the greatest display of miracles that any generation had ever seen. What happened to their faith? How did their faith fail so quickly? What happened to their very confidence in God?

I believe they missed a huge opportunity back at the Red Sea to have their faith powerfully strengthened – enough to be prepared for the soon coming testing at the waters of Marah.

You see in the midst of their storm at the Red Sea, as they were pressed up against the sea and found themselves surrounded by the angry armies of Pharaoh (with no way out) heir boldness turned to fear… Their eyes were focused on the circumstances (Pharaoh's Army) instead of on God. As a result they became angry and began murmuring…

"Then they said to Moses, because there were
no graves in Egypt, have you taken us away to
die in the wilderness? Why have you so dealt
with us, to bring us up out of Egypt? Is this not
the word that we told you in Egypt, saying, let
us alone that we may serve the Egyptians'? For
it would have been better for us to serve the
Egyptians than that we should die here in the
wilderness."
(Exodus 14:11-12)

They had lost their faith and blamed Moses for leading them out here to their "seeming" deaths… totally void in mind of all the spectacular miracles God had just performed in bringing them out of Egypt. That is what can happen to our hearts when we take our eyes off of God. Had they just responded in bold faith – perhaps they might have passed through the Red Sea on their *own faith*, instead of on the faith of Moses.

What if they had *sang* (prophetically) *The Song of Moses* and *The Song of Miriam* on **this side** of the Red Sea? Was Miriam not a prophetess??

"Then Miriam the prophetess began to…"
(Exodus 15:20)

Can you imagine what level of faith _might_ have been established in their hearts if, with their backs against the wall, (and everything on the line), they had chosen to exalt the Lord right there on the spot, with Miriam taking up the timbrels and leading the children of Israel in triumphant praise right *into the sea*, dancing, singing and declaring the faithfulness, power and Love of their God, and experienced an incredible breakthrough with a prophetic song of deliverance, and witness the mighty hand of God coming and performing the very thing they were *singing* and declaring in high praise?

Is it possible that they sang the **right song**, however they sang it on the **wrong side** of the Red Sea? What can we learn here? The Bible says:

"For whatever things were written **before** were written for <u>our</u> learning, that <u>we</u>, through the patience and comfort of the Scriptures might have hope."
(Romans 15:4)

For the Lord has given *you:*

"A Living Hope…"
(1 Peter 1:3).

In the midst of <u>your</u> storm(s), you have the very opportunity to do what the children of Israel did not… So take your eyes <u>off the storm(s)</u> themselves and all their circumstances and set them upon Jesus, by entering into high praise unto the Lord.

<u>Stay</u> in a posture of praise, worship and Intercession until you see the Salvation of the Lord. *Sing* unto the Lord <u>your</u> song, for He is <u>your</u> strength and <u>your</u> song. He <u>will</u> become your Salvation in the midst of battle – stay on Higher Ground!!

Fully *turn* your eyes upon Jesus. Look full into His wonderful face and the things (storms of this life) of earth shall grow *strangely dim*, in the Light of His Glory and Grace."

"Jesus is the Author (originator) and Finisher (brings to its fullest conclusion) of _your_ faith!" Trust Him at <u>all</u> times!

LET THE LORD BRING <u>YOU</u> THROUGH THE IMPASSABLE WAY!!

THE JUDAH SONG

"HIS ROYAL BATTLEHORSE"

Jacob loved Rachel far more than Leah, but after seven years of laboring for Rachel's hand in marriage (which Jacob made through prior agreement her father Laban), he was given the hand of Leah by technical deception. Laban claimed firstborn protocol, requiring Jacob to marry Leah *first* before marrying Rachel since Leah was the firstborn in the family.

Jacob was required to work an additional seven years to win the hand of Rachel. This new seven year period was one of great pain and anguish for Leah, knowing she was married to a man whose heart was in love with another…. She struggled and strived for his affection, longing to win Jacob's favor and attention…

The Lord saw that Leah was *unloved*, and He opened her womb. She thought if I bear him a son:

"Now therefore, my husband will love me."
(Genesis 29:31, 32)

She bore him a son and called him Reuben for "The LORD has surely looked on my affliction." But Rachel captivated Jacob's heart all those years and Leah was forced to live in a place of rejection.

So Leah bore Jacob another son, Simeon:

"Because the LORD has heard that
I *am* unloved, He has therefore

given me this son also."
(Genesis 29:33)

And so Leah named him Simeon. But even this second son did not win Jacob's heart towards Leah.

She bore Jacob a third son, Levi, again holding on to fading hope that

"Now this time my husband will become
attached to me, because I have borne him
three sons."
(Genesis 29:33)

But he did not… It was at this stage of Leah's life that she came to a place of *surrendering* her heart unto the Lord and became *willing* to live her life in thankfulness for the portion of the Lord that God had given her… Her place of surrender to the Lord was actually cultivating a deeper place of intimate praise by her *yielding* to God.

She bore Jacob a fourth son, by the name of Judah. Instead of attempting to broker yet another son to Jacob in an attempt to win his heart, she had named this child as a testimony to her heart being reconciled to the Lord,

"<u>Now</u> I will praise the LORD."
(Genesis 29:35)

Leah was transitioning in life from knowing deep rejection into a lifestyle of praise! Scripture is very clear in how much the Lord blessed her through her Judah lineage…

Judah means "Praise Yahweh" or "May Yahweh be praised". Judah held a very special place in the heart of God, but like King David, not without adversity… Though Judah was instrumental in pleading with his brothers not to kill Joseph, he eventually left his brothers to spend a season in Adullam.

There he did the unthinkable… He married a Canaanite woman and it all went downhill from there. He had several sons, the first two, Er and Onan who were so wicked and displeasing to God, He killed them both!

"But Er, Judah's firstborn, was wicked
in the sight of the LORD, and the LORD
killed him. And Judah said to Onan,
Go in to your brother's wife and marry
her, and raise up an heir to your brother.
But Onan knew that the heir would not
be his; and it came to pass, when he went
in to his brother's wife, that he emitted on
the ground, lest he should give an heir to
his brother. And the thing which he did
displeased the LORD; therefore He killed him also."
(Genesis 38:7-10)

If matters couldn't get worse, Judah ended up having sex with who he *thought* was a harlot, but in fact was his widowed daughter-in-law Tamar in disguise, (she was set out to exact vengeance upon Judah for not fulfilling his promise for her to be married to another of Judah's sons). For collateral of promised payment to her – (for services rendered), he relinquished to Tamar his signet ring, cord and staff. He did not know at that time that he had also impregnated her…

3 months later Judah is informed his daughter-in-law Tamar is pregnant outside of marriage, and being outraged, he calls for her to be brought forth and burned! When they bring Tamar forth she confirms she is pregnant and sends word to Judah that the father of this child is none other than the person

who owns these articles (as she then reveals Judah's own signet ring, cord and staff)…

"When she was brought out, she sent
to her father-in-law, saying, by the
man to whom these belong, I am with
child. And she said, please determine
whose these are—the signet and cord,
and this staff."
(Genesis 38:24, 25)

Judah is confronted by this, standing in a place of undeniable guilt, just like David did when he was confronted by the prophet Nathan. Both Judah (and his later descendant David) demanded capital punishment for the offense, yet both were hiding *secret sin*. They both had no idea there sin was about to be exposed… But the Bible says:

"You have sinned against the LORD;
and be sure…your sin *will* find you out."
(Numbers 32:23)

But through the redemptive heart of God and His *ordained plan*, Judah ends up going back to the homeland of his fathers, where he was very instrumental in the family affairs of Jacob, his Patriarch father that included playing a crucial role in that he eventually ended up leading their family down to Egypt.

Getting close to death, Jacob calls for his sons to his bedside, where he lays hands on each one of them and prophesies. When he laid hands on Judah, Jacob brought forth the most incredible prophecy that clearly revealed the destiny that God would bring to pass through the lineage of Judah…

Through Judah great praise would come forth, mighty battles would be won and even through Judah's very loins would come kings… a succession of kings… and eventually… The King of all Kings! All of this from a heartbroken woman who turned her *pain* into *praise*, and won the heart and favor of God! Through Rachel came forth Benjamin (and eventually King Saul), but through Leah came Judah and eventually King David… but then ultimately…. Jesus the Messiah!

Though Rachel was the *worldly* love story of Jacob, Leah was the *heavenly* love story of God!

"The LORD is near to those who have
a broken heart, and He saves such as
have a contrite spirit."
(Psalms 34:18)

"He **heals** the brokenhearted and
binds up their wounds.
(Psalms 147:3)

JACOB'S PROPHECY OVER JUDAH

"Judah, you are he whom your brothers
shall praise; your hand shall be on the neck
of your enemies; your father's children shall
bow down before you. Judah is a lion's whelp;
From the prey, my son, you have gone up. He
bows down, he lies down as a lion; And as a
lion, who shall rouse him? The scepter shall
not depart from Judah, nor a lawgiver from
between his feet, until **Shiloh** comes; and to
Him shall be the obedience of the people.
Binding his donkey to the vine, and his
donkey's colt to the choice vine, He washed
his garments in wine, and his clothes in the
blood of grapes. His eyes are darker than wine,

and his teeth whiter than milk.
(Genesis 49:8-12)

When the Lord stationed the tribes of Israel around the Tent of Meeting, He chose to assign the Tribe of Judah directly in front of the door of entrance to the Tent.

The tribe of Judah had grown into a mighty army by then, with scholars believing their standard (banner depicting their tribe) stationed over their encampment was that of a lion.

After Joshua died, the Israelites were being readied to fight the Canaanites. They inquired of the Lord as to which tribe to send forth *first* into battle and the Lord said:

"Now after the death of Joshua it came to
pass that the children of Israel asked the
LORD, saying, who shall be **first** to go up
for us against the Canaanites to fight against
them? And the LORD said, Judah shall go up.
Indeed I have delivered the land into his hand."
(Judges 1:1-2)

God chose the tribe of **praise** to go forth *first* into battle – and this became their standard for war…

You may be going through a difficult battle(s) right now, and the weight of adversity feels like it is overwhelming, with much pain, sorrow or stress racking your body or soul right now. As difficult as it is, you have got seize the upper hand in this fight and determine the rules of engagement! You ultimately will make the decision as to how you will move forward from this point on. If you attempt to proceed in your own strength you can end up burning up or burning out.

This very moment you do have a choice – regardless of what advantage the enemy may *seem* to have a hold of right now in your situation. Set the rules of engagement right now! You will either fight this battle upon your own *determination* and *self-effort* against the craftiness of your enemy or the excruciating circumstances <u>or</u> you could completely change the playing field right now by fully *relinquishing* this battle into the hands of Lord.

So stop! Follow the biblical mandate right now!

"Cast **ALL** of your care upon Him,
for He cares for you!"
(1 Peter 5:7)

This is not a suggestion, it is a command! You could choose to move into praise right now over the situation(s) and as you do so by releasing worship to the Lord and choosing to trust Him…*solely*… Let the outcome be of His choosing because you have relinquished it unto the Lord. Send Judah first!!

In her deep sorrow and pain, Leah came to the very point <u>you</u> might be finding yourself right now – and she finally made a heart decision…

"**NOW** I will praise the LORD."

(Genesis 29:35)

Out of that decision, the destiny of God was *opened* up to her. For out of her womb of *praise* came forth Judah (and eventually the House of David), and then ultimately a Throne without end - upon whom Jesus was to sit forever on! But out of Rachel came Benjamin and eventually… the House of Saul!

Interestingly enough, after the Judges Chapter 1 battle where the Lord first proclaimed "Send up Judah first," the very next place we see the Lord continuing to tell the tribes of Israel is:

"Then the children of Israel arose and
went up to the house of God to inquire
of God. They said, which of us shall
go up first to battle against the children
of Benjamin? The LORD said, send Judah first"
(Judges 20:18)

Whereupon we find the very tribe of Judah tribe going up
against the sons of Benjamin!

In the time when David first came out of the cave at Adullum,
his Kingship was *first* recognized by the tribe of Judah, while
all of the other tribes remained *loyal* to House of Saul, even
though he was dead!

For seven years there (continued from long standing) a war
between these tribes

"Now there was a long war between
the House of Saul and the House of
David. But David grew stronger and
stronger, and the House of Saul grew
weaker and weaker."
(2 Samuel 3:1)

One House (David) represented **praise** and being after God's
very heart. The other House (Saul) represented *self-effort* and
determination, constantly driven by *outward appearance...* and
void of a true heart connection with the Lord in their dealings.

Praise changes your atmosphere! When *you* shift *your* focus
off of *your* problems and begin to focus upon the Lord in
praise, *you* begin to transfer *your* heavy burdens upon Jesus,
and upon His Power! Take off the heavy yoke *you* have been
carrying! You were *never* meant to carry such weight upon
yourself!

Jesus Himself said:

"*Come* to Me, all *you* who labor
(in your own strength) and are
heavy laden, and I *will* give *you* rest.
Take My yoke upon *you* and *learn*
from Me, for I am gentle and lowly
in heart, and you will find rest for
your souls. For My yoke is *easy* and
My burden is *light*."
(Matthew 11:28-30)

If you can't yet begin to "*Sing Into Your Storm*", there may be more relinquishing required unto the Lord, until He has the *full weight* of *your* burden in <u>His</u> Hand. This is not an easy process – you war is real!! But as *you* truly begin to move into sincere **praise** before Him, you will begin to experience the shift and begin to feel the peace that only He can give... That peace will *become* your ability to sustain and ride out the storm in His Presence!

Right now *you* have a great opportunity to truly bring unto Jesus a "**sacrifice of praise**." It's easy to praise God when you are completely healthy, finances are there to pay your bills, the family is doing great, and no one has wronged or deeply hurt you…. It's another thing when your world has been turned upside down and anguish is all you feel, and hopelessness is all you see. To **praise** God during these circumstances requires a personal sacrifice. It takes an act of our will (heart) to lay down everything upon the altar of God… A precious friend of mine who knew much adversity in his life penned this song:

"*Come build an altar, unto the Lord,*
Return to worship and hear His Word,

And the fires of revival,
will come sweeping through your soul,
And you'll touch the Holy Presence of your God!"

Build a fresh altar of **praise** to your God in the very midst of *your* storm(s)… Lay the burdens *you're* carrying right now upon the altar and begin to **praise** the Lord! *Become* a sacrifice in **praise** and lay *your* will (and the determination to try and manage the adversity yourself) into total *surrender* upon that altar - upon the care and faithfulness of God! When the sacrifice is *acceptable*… "He is the God who answers by fire!"

Many have tried to just "praise God" in such circumstances, (without truly surrendering their hearts to Him). God Himself has spoken into such matters

"Inasmuch as these people draw *near*
with their mouths, and *honor* Me with
their lips, but they have removed their
hearts far from Me…"
(Isaiah 29:13)

If *you* will but truly surrender *your* heart in **praise** and place **all** of *your* trust in the Lord – you will *activate* the character, power and oath of God to move on *your* behalf! What better place could you be than to be leaning on the everlasting Arms? When *your* faith is set upon God and His Word – with confidence you can be **assured**:

 "Many are the afflictions of the righteous: but
the LORD delivers them out of them **ALL**!
(Psalms 34:19)

When this dynamic truth becomes a reality, *you* will possess a maturity level and empowered faith that will be your strength is the storms and battles that will continue to come into your life at various times, throughout the rest of _your_ life. _You_ can become a powerful vessel in the hands of God!

"For the LORD of hosts will visit His flock,
the house of Judah, and will make them
as His **_royal horse in the battle_**. From him
comes the Cornerstone, from him the tent peg,
from him the battle bow, from him every ruler
together. They shall be like **mighty men**, who
tread down their enemies in the mire of the streets
in the battle. They shall fight because the LORD is
with _them_, and the riders on horses shall be put
to shame."
(Zechariah 10:3-5)

_"Send Judah first, and the battle will be won,
send Judah first, and the foes are overcome,
giving praise to the Father, and Glory to the Son,
send Judah first!"_

Your victory through **high praise** isn't just for you! As you press through the heavy storm(s) in life, what God is developing in you, He will surely use down the course of _your_ journey as a powerful testimony to encourage, strengthen and bless other people, your church – and even other cities!

Praise is the way _through_ your storm(s)… God will reveal facets of His character, faithfulness, and mercy in ways you _never_ would have come to know, any other way - aside from walking through a trial by fire.

Andrae Crouch, one of the most prolific and heart stirring songwriters of our time, deeply blessed the entire Body of Christ with incredible songs of **praise** (_To God Be The Glory_), and songs of victory and triumph (_His Blood Will Never Lose Its Power_) etc.

These and many others came to Andrae by way of the severe storms that came in his life. He wrote *songs* that were birthed from great adversity, *songs* that God ending up using to bless and encourage countless millions! Andrae knew there was Divine purpose (and opportunity) in each of his storms. His song *Through It All* really declares that:

"...But in every situation, God gave Blessed consolation, that <u>my trials had only come to make me strong</u>,

So I <u>thank God for the mountains</u>, I <u>thank God for the valleys</u>, I <u>thank God for every storm</u>, <u>He's brought me through</u>,

For if I never had a problem, I wouldn't know that He could solve them, and I'd <u>never</u> know what <u>faith in God</u> can do."

Through it all, through it all, I've learned to <u>trust in Jesus</u>, I've learned to <u>trust in God</u>, through it all, through it all... I have learned to <u>depend</u> upon His Word."

When facing storms in <u>your</u> life, if <u>you</u> would but posture your heart to trust God, and maintain focus on Him, and to begin *seeing* the storm with the understanding of Divine purpose...

<u>You</u> will become His Royal Battlehorse – one whom God can use mightily for His Glory!

JUDAH – HIS ROYAL BATTLEHORSE

THE SONG OF JEHOSHAPHAT

"THE BATTLE BELONGS TO THE LORD"

Jehoshaphat was a descendant King from the line of David, of the tribe of Judah (Praise). He was a godly King, set upon cleansing his nation of idolatry. He dispatched the Levite priests across the land to teach the people the Law.

But along the path of his kingship, he made a serious mistake and aligned with King Ahab (Jezebel's husband) and trusted the multitude of Ahab's prophets when kings of Israel & Judah inquired as to whether they should go to war and capture Ramoth-Gilead. Ahab's prophets all said "go to war", but in getting a second opinion, there was a proven (accurate) prophet in the land named Micaiah who told them the campaign would end in utter ruin...

They went to war at Ramoth-Gilead and in deed suffered great loss, disgrace and disaster. If only he had listened to the *true* prophetic voice of Micaiah… Afterwards, another true prophet of the Lord named Jehu came and reproached him for the course he had been taking:

"When Jehoshaphat king of Judah returned
safely to his palace in Jerusalem, Jehu the
seer, the son of Hanani, went out to meet him
and said to the king, should you help the
wicked and love those who hate the LORD?
Because of this, the wrath of the LORD is
upon you. There is, however, some good in you,
 for you have rid the land of the Asherah poles
and set your heart on seeking God."

(2 Chronicles 19:1-3)

This caused King Jehoshaphat to return to a vigorous campaign of displacing all forms of idolatry from the peoples, deepening their interest back to the worship of the one true God and instilling the integrity of righteous government.

But one day, Jehoshaphat got news that a very dark and powerful storm was about to head his way. An unavoidable storm… The Moabites, Ammonites and other surrounding kingdoms had formed a confederacy to come against Jehoshaphat in war. It was only a matter of time before the hordes of hell would march towards him… What could he do? He could have tried to summon up all his army and to try and plot a strategic warfare against their army (that vastly outnumbered them)... But this would have been done in his own strength and wisdom. So what did he do?

King Jehoshaphat did exactly what _you_ and I should do when storms begin form and head directly towards us and when the appearance of the enemy has unleashed the hordes of hell against you, your family or friends, church or nation…

"And Jehoshaphat feared, and set himself
to seek the LORD, and proclaimed a fast
throughout all Judah. So Judah gathered
together to _ask_ for help from the LORD; with
all the cities of Judah they came to _seek_ the LORD.
(2 Chronicles 20:3, 4)

He _chose_ to _fast_ and _pray_ and _seek_ the Lord. His eyes were _set_ upon God – and _not_ upon his enemy! In corporate intercession King Jehoshaphat stood up and declared in the midst of the assembly of Judah from the House of the Lord:

"…O LORD God of our fathers, are You
not God in Heaven, and do You not rule
over *all* the kingdoms of the nations, and
in Your hand is there not power and might,
so that no one is able to withstand You?
Are You not our God, who drove out the
inhabitants of this land before Your people
Israel, and gave it to the descendants of
Abraham Your friend forever?
(2 Chronicles 20:6, 7)

He called upon the name of God, *reminding* God of His *faithfulness* and His *promise* to Israel. He put the outcome of the battle into the hands of God – this is **_exactly_** what we must **learn** to do in our battle(s) – even when the circumstances of the storm seem *overwhelming* to us. This is where true faith is developed and where ultimate dependency upon God can be exercised so that you can *prevail*. And we know this by the Word of God:

"And this is the victory that has overcome the world
even our faith."
(1 John 5:4)

Their posture of heart before the Lord *empowered* God to move on their behalf… The Lord was about to do a mighty thing… To show Himself strong on behalf of hearts who showed themselves loyal to Him *through* faith and trust… so God could demonstrate the power of Heaven being released because they *sought* (inquired of) the Lord their God first!

At that moment, the Spirit fell upon a prophet named Jahaziel, (who was Zechariah's son). He spoke under a powerful prophetic unction from the Lord and proclaimed:

"Listen, all you of Judah and you
inhabitants of Jerusalem, and you,
King Jehoshaphat! Thus says the
LORD to you: Do not be *afraid* nor
dismayed because of this great multitude,
for the _battle is not yours, but God's_!
Tomorrow go down against them. They
will surely come up by the Ascent of Ziz,
and you will find them at the end of the
brook before the Wilderness of Jeruel.
You will **not** _need_ to fight in this battle.
Position yourselves, stand still and
see the salvation of the LORD, who is
with you, O Judah and Jerusalem!
Do not *fear* or be *dismayed*;
tomorrow go out against them, for
the LORD **is** with you."
(2 Chronicles 20:15-17)

Once they heard this, they *knew* - the blueprint of Heaven for the battle had been given by God to King Jehoshaphat... There is a blueprint in Heaven for _you_ too – God has a plan for your passage and victory – so don't take matters into *your* own hands and become *overwhelmed* by your battle(s). God **is** Faithful! _Your_ job is to earnestly *seek* the Lord – and **not** move *forth* until _you_ too **know** His battle plans!

"He *bowed* his head with his face to the
ground, and all Judah and the inhabitants

of Jerusalem *bowed* before the LORD, *worshiping*
the LORD. Then the Levites of the children of
the Kohathites and of the children of the Korahites
stood up to **praise** the LORD God of Israel with
voices loud and high.
(2 Chronicles 20:18, 19)

What an amazing revelation! ***The battle is not ours*** – the battle
belongs to the Lord! Yes, the battle belongs to the Lord – but
only when we *actually* give it over to Him completely and
unconditionally! The problem with the failure of so many of
the previous battles in our lives is that each of us became so
overcome with *fear* or *anger* and such… that we *tried* to engage
the battle by ourselves, attempting to prevail through our *own*
strength and determination.

On the morning of battle, King Jehoshaphat does an
incredible thing… He reveals an even *greater* truth about the
ways of God… Not only does the battle belong to the Lord, in
this instance they are told not only don't they need to fight…
But that the ultimate war strategy there was to just *send forth*
praise on to the battlefield!

"Hear me, O Judah and you inhabitants
of Jerusalem: **Believe** in the LORD your God,
and you shall be established; **believe** His
prophets, and you shall prosper! And when
he had consulted with the people, he appointed
those who should *sing* to the LORD, and who
should **praise** the beauty of holiness… They
went out before the army and were *singing*:
Praise the LORD, For His mercy *endures* forever."
(2 Chronicles 20:20, 21)

Talk about *singing into your storm*! It was a great and mighty victory that day, for the Lord Himself routed the armies of Moab and Ammon and the other surrounding nations. The Lord so utterly confused them enemy that they ended up killing each other! But the actual routing took place *because* of their obedience to follow God's plan… To worship the Lord!

"Now when they began to *sing* and to **praise**,
the LORD set ambushes against the people of
Ammon, Moab, and Mount Seir, who had
come against Judah; and they were defeated.
For the people of Ammon and Moab stood up
against the inhabitants of Mount Seir to utterly
kill and destroy them. And when they had made
an end of the inhabitants of Seir, they helped to
destroy one another."
(2 Chronicles 20:22, 23)

There is a stark contrast here between that of Jehoshaphat's battle and the battle of the children of Israel against the Egyptians at the Red Sea. In both *storms* of battle, the people of God are completely surrounded by their enemies who are bent on killing them. The potential for great *fear* to set in and completely inundate *both* camps was very real! The Lord's plan in both battles was demonstrate His great love for Israel, (His special treasure), through His *mighty* power, and to compel them to *fully* trust in Him, so that they might learn to be able to **worship** Him with all of their hearts!

In both events, (though separated by about 500 years), each had a godly leader out in front. Both generations were given the same charge:

Moses At The Red Sea

"Do **not** be *afraid*. **Stand still and see the Salvation of the Lord**, which He will accomplish for you today. For the Egyptians whom you see today, you shall see again no more forever. The Lord <u>will</u> fight for you, and you shall hold your peace."
(Exodus 14:13, 14)

Jehoshaphat At Jerusalem

"You will **not** need to fight in this battle. Position yourselves, **stand still and see the salvation of the LORD**, who is with you, O Judah and Jerusalem!"
(2 Chronicles 20:17)

In the case at the Red Sea, the children of Israel let *fear* set in (even though the charge to their faith was to **not** be *afraid*). This led to *panic* and *anger* in which they ended up bringing harsh accusations against Moses. They became beset with *unbelief* until the faith of Moses stretched out his staff and brought forth their great deliverance! *Fear* is the *fastest* path to unbelief. No matter what kind of storm(s) might be before <u>you</u> right now, *fear* is usually one of the first visitor's to arrive at the door of <u>your</u> heart… to try and *overthrow* your faith!

As Jehoshaphat stood in the assembly of his people at Jerusalem, he led forth corporate intercession, which caused the Spirit of the Lord to fall upon the peoples. The Spirit of prophecy brought forth the mandate from the Lord:

"Listen, all you of Judah and you inhabitants of Jerusalem, and you,

King Jehoshaphat! Thus says the LORD
to you: **Do not be afraid nor dismayed**
because of this great multitude, for the
battle is **not** yours, but God's."
(2 Chronicles 20:15)

At that very moment what differentiated these two events
was that King Jehoshaphat and all the people _bowed_ on their
faces before the Lord.

"And Jehoshaphat _bowed_ his head
with _his_ face to the ground, and _all_ Judah
and the inhabitants of Jerusalem _bowed_
before the LORD, **worshiping** the LORD."
(2 Chronicles 20:18)

In faith and reverence toward their God, they _chose_ to place
their confidence in the Lord… They _chose_ faith instead of fear!
They surrendered their battle (storm) into the hands of God!

This is **exactly** what the Lord would have of all who are
standing before a great storm(s) right now! _Bow_ before the
Lord and surrender _your_ storm(s) into the hands of God right
now. Turn your gaze upon the loveliness of Jesus and release
everything to Him. Let His peace engulf you right now – it will
surely come **if** you **sincerely** surrender… unconditionally!

Many people will say in the midst of their storm(s) they are
facing a great trial, affliction or tragedy i.e. "I am _facing_ cancer"
or "I am _facing_ foreclosure on my home etc." The greatest
problem with this is that you are simply _facing_ the wrong
direction! Instead of _facing_ your problem, turn _your_ face
towards Jesus!" Take _your_ eyes off of the storm(s) itself and
set it upon Jesus!"

In Matthew 14 the disciples were all in a boat late into the fourth watch of the night. A great storm came upon them and tossed their boat to and fro, and they were all *afraid*. Suddenly they see Jesus literally walking on the water towards them!

Jesus does the most incredible thing…. He speaks to them and the first words out of His mouth is this:

"Be of good cheer! **IAM**; do *not* be afraid."
(Matthew 14:27)

He revealed Himself to them in the midst of their storm as the **IAM**! In Greek the word is *ego eimi*. Jesus used the exact same word when He spoke to the Pharisees and declared:

"Jesus said to them, Most assuredly, I say
to you, before Abraham was, **IAM**."
(John 8:58)

The Pharisees were so outraged at Him claiming to be **IAM**, they picked up stones and hurled them at Him! So here is Jesus showing up in the midst of their storm and manifesting Himself as the **IAM**!

Jesus is the **IAM** in *your* life and in *your* storms!! He is the all *Sufficient One*, the *Un-Created One*, and the *Eternal* God. He is more than worthy of *your* trust... of *your* complete faith!

The essence of faith in God can be described as the entire leaning of one's self (mind, will and emotions) upon the firm foundation of God's Goodness, Wisdom & Power – like leaning so far slanted against a wall that if the wall moved you would absolutely fall - resting *all* upon God's Attributes:

God's Goodness... God is Love... pure Love. He demonstrated His Love for us in that while we were yet still sinners - Christ Died for us. The Father sent His only Son to make the ultimate sacrifice for us – that we might be adopted back into the Royal Family of God. Everything God does is for our greatest good. *Father knows best*!!

God's Wisdom… God is omniscience, that is, He knows everything there is to know. There is nothing that He doesn't know. So when He makes a plan or a decision concerning *your* life – He has done it from the standpoint of knowing *every* possible factor. He has considered everything and every outcome concerning *you*, so *you* can absolutely **rely** on His plans and His judgements (which are all together righteous…)

God's Power. God is omnipotent, that is, *all powerful*… there is nothing He can't do by His Mighty Power. What is impossible with man *is* possible with God!

So just think of it…. *You* are putting your complete trust and faith upon One who has steadfastly proven His Love for *you*. With His *all knowing* Wisdom, has a plan for *your* life to give *you* a hope and a future that can be absolutely relied… We are talking about the One who knows the end from the beginning! In the midst of His great Love and Wisdom, this One also has the very power to **protect** *you*, to **lead** *you*, to **provide** for *you*, to **save** *you* and to bring forth the fullest conclusion (and harvest) from *your* life!

Yet sometimes the storm(s) in our life *seem* so overwhelming that for us to *fully* surrender to the Lord and letting Him take over the battle seems like the most difficult thing we will ever do. Why? Because we are *afraid*! It is almost like dangling off the edge of a high cliff and the Lord is saying "Let go child, I will catch you!" But the *height* of the cliff and the *fear* of falling is so exasperating we are *gripped* with *fright*! We are holding on for dear life, when in reality we should be letting go for dear life!

"**Letting go and letting God**" is one of the most life changing experiences you will ever have. When you finally pass the test of faith through a storm, by *fully* releasing it to the Lord (no matter the outcome the Lord has determined), *you* will learn a valuable revelation about the character of God. He is faithful! Your victory in faith from that storm will go a long way in helping prepare you for future storms in your life!

We will mature in the Lord (through experience) as we learn how to release **praise** in our storms, and *fully* lean upon the Lord! There is no other way… Our relinquishment of the situation can be in the form declaring unto the Lord - through *prayer* and *praise* – His awesome faithfulness and the trustworthiness of our God <u>over</u> your storm(s)!! Then waiting upon the Lord for His battle plan to come forth…

Sing into your storm(s)!

"The LORD *is* <u>*my*</u> strength and <u>*my song,*</u>
and He has become <u>*my*</u> salvation."
(Psalms 118:14)

"I will praise You, for You have answered me, and have become <u>*my*</u> salvation!"
(Psalms 118:21)

As in the days of Moses and Jehoshaphat – so now for <u>*you*</u>:

<u>**"Stand still and see the Salvation of the Lord!!"**</u>

THE BATTLE
BELONGS TO THE LORD

1 Samuel 17

CALL UPON THE GOD
OF ANGEL ARMIES!!
THE LORD OF HOSTS

"ENTERING LAMENTATION WORSHIP"

Lament is an essential ingredient in *honest* faith. Lamentation worship is bringing to God your true pain, sorrow or suffering while still choosing to worship the King. It constitutes encountering a Divine embrace with the living God - from the midst of <u>your</u> deep and personal anguish, and the bearing your heart and soul unto God, allowing Him to receive your deep burden...

Many think if we force ourselves to enter this kind of place in worship that God is responsible to lift all of the pain from you. The most *honest* answer is that is not always true…

Jesus knew his friend Lazarus was going to die, but he also knew that it would not be permanent and that the Son of God would be glorified through it. He told His disciples:

"This sickness is not unto death,
but for the glory of God, that the
Son of God may be glorified through it."
(John 11:4)

So when Jesus first got word that Lazarus was sick unto death, instead of rushing over there to "heal" him, He chose to remain in the place He was at for two more days… He *knew* the will of the Father and <u>only</u> did that which the Father directed Him to do at all times…

"Finally He came near Bethany, Lazarus sister Mary met Jesus; then, when Mary came where Jesus was, and saw Him, she fell down at His feet, saying to Him, "Lord, if You had been here, my brother would not have died. Therefore, when Jesus saw her weeping, and the Jews who came with her weeping, He *groaned* in the spirit and was *troubled*. And He said, "Where have you laid him?" They said to Him, "Lord, come and see. **Jesus wept.**"
(John 11:32-35)

On one hand, Jesus knew the will of the Father and that this death was only temporary, but on the other hand Jesus was so moved with compassion and the weeping of Mary and her companions that it caused Him to embrace their deep sorrow, and caused Him to weep too!

When we come to the Lord in lamentation (in pain, sorrow, suffering, vexation of heart, soul and or body), the Lord may embrace our anguish and even *weep* with us, because He loves us and cares for us so much. But the Lord is intent on fulfilling His will – the will of the Father and will only grant what the Father says - even though He has joined us in our pain.

I pray you can grasp this about our God. He is so tender hearted towards us and all that we go through, with a heart longing to heal, deliver, encourage, strengthen, and miraculously provide – but not beyond His will in the long run, since He knows what's best at all times. God doesn't always say yes…

Sometimes He says wait…

Sometimes He says no…

****

The Author wishes to share one of the most heartfelt, and impacting testimonies you will have ever heard. Please believe me when I tell you that I struggled greatly as to whether to share this or not. When I am done sharing this story, I think you will understand my reluctance to share it, but also understand why I felt it had to be shared….

I chose to share it because of the great encouragement it will bring to many who are standing in the biggest storm(s) of their life right now, and for the deeper insight it will provide people into the character, nature and the Love that God has for you.

My wife Betty and I were married in 1992. Within a few months she became pregnant, and on February 28, 1993 we had a beautiful little girl. We named her Rachel Ann-Marie. She was the most beautiful baby! She was our *little lamb*. (Rachel means lamb).

Since my wife and I both had full time jobs, we shared early morning responsibilities with Rachel Ann-Marie (that is Ann-Marie… a hyphen… something we used to joke about all the time)...

In the morning Betty would bathe and feed Rachel and then I would drive her about 15 miles to our preferred care provider.

Those mornings driving along with my daughter in her car seat next to me in the front seat of the car were so special…

I was the happiest (and proudest dad in the world). During our drive each day, Rachel and I would listen to FOCUS ON THE FAMILY on the radio with Dr. James Dobson (since I was going to become the world's greatest dad)…

Several months into our daily journey, the radio program did a special series on the stories behind many of the great hymns.

One hymn in particular, I had heard at least part of the story beforehand which impacted me so deeply, that I was really looking forward to hearing the *entire* story… It was the story of Horatio Spafford, and the great hymn he wrote called "It is well with my Soul."

Horatio was one of the wealthiest businessmen at the turn of the century in Chicago, Illinois. A devout Christian, great husband, father and loved by many for his generosity.

He had a son who became gravely ill. As a righteous man before the Lord, he pleaded incessantly for the Lord to heal his boy. Horatio was a mature Christian in the faith and I have no doubt that he possessed the faith and confidence in God to see his son healed. But the Lord did not heal his son – he died.

Grief-stricken by the tragic loss, and in trying to console his wife and four daughters. He arranged for the family to go on a ship cruise over to Europe to process their grief and take time for his family to heal.

Just days before the voyage, a well-known chapter in history occurred… Old Lady O'Leary's cow kicked over a lantern in a barn, which caused the great Chicago fire that burned up almost all of the Chicago waterfront.

Horatio owned significant portions of property all along the waterfront of Chicago – and many of his buildings and properties were lost.

As I listened to the story, I marveled about this man's faith. Here he had lost his own precious son, while as a righteous man crying out to God for a miracle. And now almost all of his property and holdings were destroyed. Why do such terrible things happen to such godly and devout people?

The City Recorder came to Horatio and told him it was imperative that he be at a special town council meeting that was scheduled in a few days… At this meeting they were going to redraw property lines for all of the downtown waterfront areas of Chicago. They were prompted to do this because all the deeds, plats and maps etc. as City Hall had been burned up in the fire as well. The City Recorder strongly urged Horatio to be at this meeting because his property holdings in that area were vast and the clerk could not guarantee he would be afforded back the entirety of his properties if he was not there to represent his holdings…

Horatio realized he had to be at that meeting, yet the voyage was scheduled to embark earlier than that so he arranged for his wife and four daughters to keep the cruise date and then he would join them in Europe on a later cruise *after* he took care of the property re-distribution.

Before he could leave on his cruise, he received an urgent telegram from his wife… The ship they were on was struck by another ship, and 226 people drowned, including Horatio's four daughters… Only his wife survived. He made plans to join her as quickly as possible in Europe.

I was undone by the story as I drove to our care provider's, listening to this unbelievable story of the back to back tragedies of this man – and of his persevering faith. To even lose a son would be devastating enough… but to then lose almost all your property and wealth.

And now to learn that he has also lost all four of his daughters as well? I was in tears as I listened to this story. I remember looking at my beautiful little lamb Rachel Ann-Marie (that's Ann-Marie with a hyphen…) and just tried to imagine the deep pain and sorrow I would feel if I ever lost something so precious – and to think this man had lost 5 Rachel's….

Little did I know at that very moment, the Lord was actually preparing my heart through this incredible story – because in a few weeks, I too, was about to lose my little lamb – Rachel Ann-Marie…

On board the ship and heading to Europe, Horatio asked the Captain of the ship if he would come and wake him up when the ship passed over the sea grave of his daughters (since the ships always followed the same exact routes).

The early hours of the morning, the Captain came and got Horatio and let him know they would be passing over that area where his daughter's ship had gone down within a matter of minutes. Horatio went up on deck and looked over board into the cold chilling waters, knowing his precious four daughters had drowned right there in those waters…

In the midst of the deepest pain and sorrow anybody could ever imagine, he went back down to his cabin that morning, and penned the words to what would become one of the greatest hymns of all time – written from a heart in

lamentation and worship unto God – all at the same time…
this is *true* lamentation worship…

It Is Well With My Soul

1. When peace, like a river, attendeth my way,
   When sorrows like sea billows roll;
   Whatever my lot, Thou hast taught me to say,
   It is well, it is well with my soul.

   o *Refrain:*
     It is well with my soul,
     It is well, it is well with my soul.

2. Though Satan should buffet, though trials should come,
   Let this blest assurance control,
   That Christ hath regarded my helpless estate,
   And hath shed His own blood for my soul.

3. My sin—oh, the bliss of this glorious thought!—
   My sin, not in part but the whole,
   Is nailed to the cross, and I bear it no more,
   Praise the Lord, praise the Lord, O my soul!

4. For me, be it Christ, be it Christ hence to live:
   If Jordan above me shall roll,
   No pang shall be mine, for in death as in life
   Thou wilt whisper Thy peace to my soul.

5. But, Lord, 'tis for Thee, for Thy coming we wait,
   The sky, not the grave, is our goal;
   Oh, trump of the angel! Oh, voice of the Lord!
   Blessed hope, blessed rest of my soul!

6. And Lord, haste the day when the faith shall be sight,
   The clouds be rolled back as a scroll;
   The trump shall resound, and the Lord shall descend,
   Even so, it is well with my soul.

I was so utterly overcome with emotion as I heard the radio announcer recite the words to this song. I couldn't even imagine the level of pain this man must have felt, how on earth with that level of grief and sorrow he could have brought himself to write such an incredible *song* of praise, and *song* of hope at such a difficult moment.

Well, I was to find out…

I have always been a fervent worshipper out of deep gratitude for the enormous debt that the Lord had paid on my behalf. I had become a subscriber to the Integrity Hosanna Music Club in which I received their newest praise and worship cassette every 8 weeks. At the exact same time as I was so richly enjoying the "Focus on the Family's" stories behind the great hymn's, I had also *just* received Hosanna's brand new album for that time period which was called "God Will Make a Way" by Don Moen… It was such beautiful, encouraging and uplifting music to listen to, especially for people who were going through a difficult time in their lives…

The title song had been written by Don Moen to his Sister-In-Law after he had learned that their 8 year old son had been killed in a tragic car accident. Here are the words to that song:

"God will make a way,
Where there seems to be no way.
He works in ways we cannot see,
He will make a way for me.

He will be my guide,
Hold me closely to His side.
With love and strength for each new day,
He will make a way, He will make a way.

By a roadway in the wilderness, He'll lead me,
And rivers in the desert will I see.
Heaven and Earth will fade, but His Word will still remain.
And He will do something new today."

Around 11am in the morning, a few weeks later at work, the office secretary ran up to me "You have got to get over to your babysitter's house – your daughter is in an ambulance there."

I ran out the door in an instant, driving at high speed to get to our daycare provider. When I arrived on the scene there were many first responder vehicles of every kind there and over a hundred people standing by in a swarm. My wife arrived minutes later.

One of the EMT'S told us the babysitter had laid her down for a nap and upon checking on her latr discovered she was not breathing. They had put her on a ventilator, but told us that the machine was doing all of the breathing at that point.

I immediately went boldly before the Throne of Grace in a time of need and **pleaded** with my Lord and Savior to spare her life…. I *knew* I had the faith to see a miracle right then….

We waited and waited, praying continuously… After about 45 minutes I couldn't stand it any longer. I popped my head in the front cab of the emergency EMT truck. I saw 4 or 5 EMT'S working on her. I recognized the lead EMT in the group trying to resuscitate her – he went to our church.

I didn't say a word so as not to distract them – but he looked up at me, knowing what a crying father wanted to know… one way or another… and with the deepest gesture of sympathy and sadness for me – he didn't say a word – he just shook his head back and forth as to say "I'm sorry."

I will forever remember that moment… it was like a sword piercing my heart… I went and put my arms around my wife to break the most horrific news… We wept profusely…

My Pastor was already zooming to the scene having learned of the emergency. On the way there he was praying for us (already knowing she was likely not going to make it). As he prayed, he asked the Lord "What can I say to them?" Then the Lord spoke to him on the spot and told him "Tell them that David has a son…"

After an extensive interview with the local sheriff and other law enforcement personnel (standard procedure), my wife and I left the scene to go home – we just wanted to be alone. I knew I needed to call my family and let them know that our precious Rachel Ann-Marie was gone…

With deep heaviness, I relayed the story to my brother who had answered the phone, (who is also a Christian), and was quite startled when the first thing he said to me was "You know David had a son…" I was stunned…

In less than 90 minutes, twice, we were given the same word. We knew there must be application for us in this Bible story so we looked it up and read about it.

The story is found in the book of 2 Samuel 12:16-23.

What particularly caught our attention was what King David did *after* he had learned that his child had died:

"Then David got up from the floor,
washed himself, put lotions on, and
changed his clothes. Then he went into
the LORD's house to worship."
(2 Samuel 12:20)

We *knew* this was what we needed to do too – even in the midst of the deepest grief and sorrow our broken hearts have ever known… We *knew* that God was speaking to <u>us</u> through this story of David…

Within that hour, we had to go to the Mortuary and meet with the Funeral Director. It was a very late Friday afternoon. Normally about this time, we would be trying to choose between Chinese food or pizza for dinner and what movie to rent etc. This day were being show different coffins and choice of fabric liners for the casket etc. and being asked what final dress we would want her to wear and if we would like to have a bonnet etc… it was absolutely devastating…

 My wife was adamant that we would not bury our daughter in the most beautiful red velvet dress she had recently bought for her (a dress she was going to wear for the first time at Christmas). So we went and bought a dress for the funeral.

We never got that first Christmas with our little lamb… She was born on February 28th, 1993 and died on June 25th. It was later determined she had died from *crib death* or Sudden Infant Death Syndrome (SIDS).

Remembering what David had did at the loss of his baby, we called the Pastor and asked if we could have access to the Church Saturday night (alone) to follow the example of David and worship the Lord (though we didn't know how we could bring ourselves to do it - being in such pain)…

We entered the Sanctuary late in the evening and were alone before the Lord. We sat before His Presence, walked around the room, determined to try and lift up **praise** to Him for Rachel's life, and thank Him for the four wonderful months we got to enjoy being her parents… It was <u>so</u> difficult to do…

****

<u>Author's Note:</u>

Again what happened next is a matter of testimony… **<u>Please</u>** believe me when I say I am struggling greatly, even at this very moment to share with you what happened… We have only shared this testimony with a very few select friends up to this moment...

There will be many readers who hear this story and instantly believe in their hearts that it was absolutely through the Grace and Glory of God concerning what transpired... But others will be more doubtful and skeptical, and there will be some who will clearly not believe what occurred... I just want to say here and now - I truly honor <u>all</u> of you, and totally respect *whatever* position you may take on this story… This story needs to be judged on a person by person basis…

Before I share this, I want to make it as clear as possible one more time… the <u>*only*</u> reason my heart compels me to share this story is for the sake of the many readers who will be forever impacted in their hearts as they see what God can do, and how He comes and comforts _us_ in the midst of _our_ grief and sorrow. It is for _their_ benefit I share this amazing story…

The Author's Testimony:

God's Presence was there in the Sanctuary, and tremendous Grace filled the atmosphere. My wife and I were in different parts of the Sanctuary, walking, sitting, kneeling etc, but after about 45 minutes, we both somehow ended up coming before the altar (it was not planned by either of us). We both were kneeling side by side before the altar, both of us weeping, forcing ourselves to bring forth **praise** from a well of tears…

Both my wife and I had our eyes closed, still kneeling side by side before the altar. We were both sobbing, continuing to try and pour forth worship to the Lord. While my eyes were still yet _closed_, it was as if I turned my heard in the Spirit (not physically) over to my right side to look upon my wife… As I did I was profoundly and utterly amazed at what I saw… I literally saw my wife holding Rachel Ann-Marie in her arms! Rachel was absolutely beautiful!! It wasn't her physical body – it was her spirit… translucent, pure and glorious… Words do not do justice to describe her beauty in that state…

I was sure it must be some kind of vision I was having. My eyes were still completely closed (physically). I was undone! I had no precedent by which to judge or understand what I was experiencing… I didn't want to open my natural eyes as I was afraid of losing _sight_ in seeing my precious daughter this last time, but my natural mind kept beckoning me to look…

And then I opened my _natural_ eyes and looked over to my wife, and there she was – I was _astonished_ to literally see my wife Betty holding the living and glorious spirit of our beloved child – cradled in her arms! Only it _wasn't_ just me seeing this, or having some kind of personal vision... My wife _too_ was literally and physically beholding the exact same experience and holding Rachel in her arms!!!

Indescribable!! How could this be? I searched my wealth of the knowledge of Scripture in trying to understand this Grace beyond imagination! The Lord then spoke clearly to my heart that we had about 15 minutes to behold our precious daughter. He made it known that when the time was up, we were to lift her up and release her into the eternal House of the Lord (Heaven) to dwell forever… into the arms of Jesus!

In that moment, we told our daughter how much we loved her, as the moments speeded by so fast. When the Lord signaled that it was time, I laid my hand upon her head and prayed a prayer of releasing her into Heaven… When I finished, we both lifted her up before the Lord, and in a moment she was lifted up from us - ever to be with Jesus!

It would have been one thing if it had just been me experiencing this in the Spirit with my eyes closed… but to open my physical eyes and not only _see_ it happening for real but for my wife to be experiencing the _exact_ same thing _too_ is a completely different subject… We had confirmation…

"For out of the mouth of two or three
witnesses are matters established…"
(2 Corinthians 13:1)

In establishing this testimony, I have asked my beloved wife to share her testimony about this encounter also…

The Author's Wife Testimony:

When we lost our daughter Rachel Ann-Marie to SIDS, Sudden Infant Death Syndrome, it was a like a nightmare we couldn't wake up from. God had, from the beginning of her life, impressed upon me that she was His daughter and that we were to hold her with an open hand. We she died, were naturally in shock, yet at the very same time we were covered by the Grace of God.

Since we had received two confirmations about the same story of King David losing his child – within the first couple hours of our daughters passing, we decided to "Do what King David did." So we looked up the story to review what King David did when his child died. He cleaned himself up, put on fresh clothes, and went to the Tabernacle to worship God. So this is what we did. We arranged with our Pastor to go to the church for an hour after the worship team finished their practice late Saturday night, so we could worship God. We took a CD (or cassette) player and music to play while we *tried* to focus on God and His goodness...

During this time of worship, I longed to hold my baby just one more time… While worshipping, I extended my arms out in front of me, while resting on my lap. As I did this, I could feel my baby in my arms. She was not there in the natural, but she was there in spirit! Within minutes my husband opened his eyes and he could see her very clearly. I told my husband he could touch her head from my left side! It was awesome! God gave me the desire of my heart. Wow! Words cannot express my gratitude to God! A couple of days before her death, an angel had appeared at the end of her crib. Later I knew why… Betty Johnson

We **chose** to *force* ourselves to worship the Lord in the darkest hour of our lives. It was clear to us having received twice the word about what King David did in the loss of his child. In so doing, the Lord decided to bless us beyond anything we could have ever expected or imagined. We *broke through* the wall of despair through lamentation worship into an incredible place before the Lord, a place where the Lord was so moved by our determination to worship Him in lamentation that He did a wondrous thing!

The kindness of the Lord to allow my wife to hold her child one last time (knowing that even in the months and years to come how much her arms would ache to hold her…). This opened up a facet of God's Love and Compassion beyond anything we have ever known about Him…

In lamentation worship, we lift our pain and sorrow up unto God, the one who is well acquainted with all of our griefs and sorrows. In the loss of Rachel Ann-Marie, the question of 'Why God?" continually tried to dominant our minds and our hearts. We could have spent all of our energy on that subject alone… The one thing we were able to determine in the midst of this great tragedy was that "Though we may _never_ understand God's reasoning for this during our lifetime – the one solid, undisputable fact remains… God is trustworthy… That is – He is _worthy_ of ALL of our trust."

No matter what kind of storm(s) you are encountering right now, God has proven over and over in our lives that He is _worthy_ of us placing them into His hands. Not only is He completely trustworthy – He is also _faithful_…

God _makes_ a way where there seems to be no way… If we would but _only_ trust Him completely. He doesn't necessarily make the pain and sorrow go away instantly, but imparts Grace to walk a sometimes hard road.

In lamentation worship we have to overcome the anguish of our soul to press through to God. Many of the Psalms were written with this in mind:

"Why are you cast down, O my soul?
And why are you disquieted within me?
Put your hope in God, for I shall yet
praise Him…"
(Psalms 42:5)

God _will_ make a way… I am so thankful how the Lord prepared my heart for such grief and loss by leading me weeks beforehand to hear the story of Horatio Spafford and "It Is Well With My Soul," and Don Moen's _song_ "God Will Make A Way." That became the theme of our daughter's funeral. Both _songs_ were sung at the funeral service.

But what happened next is yet _another_ testimony into the amazing _lovingkindness_ of the Lord.

Rachel Ann-Marie's death occurred on a Friday around the lunch hour. By the time we ended up meeting with the Funeral Director to plan her funeral - it was at the end of the day. So there was no time to purchase a cemetery plot and have it dug.

The funeral was set for the following Monday so we chose to forego the graveside portion of the service since the cemetery plot wasn't prepared yet. It was agreed that the service would be on Monday and then on Tuesday, just the Funeral Director and I would go up to bury our daughter's remains.

What we didn't expect was that my wife's sister flew into town late Monday night (too late for the funeral that day). The next morning as I was preparing to leave to go up to the cemetery, my Sister-In-Law asked me "Would you mind if I went up with you – since I missed the funeral, this would help with closure for me?" I agreed…

It all happened so quickly, one moment burying her and then the next minute seeing the guys recover the plot with grass and place flowers on top. I was just getting ready to leave when again my Sister-In-Law asked me very tenderly "It is very difficult for me to ask you this but - would you please allow me to take a few pictures of you standing over her grave… you may never want to look at those pictures again but unless I take them, you will never have that opportunity."

So again, I agreed to have her take them. I stood over my daughter's grave, it was around the noon hour on a bright and sunny day in June. She took perhaps 12 pictures.

As she was finishing the last pictures, I somehow gained a deeper insight into the reality of the situation – that my daughter was now in Heaven and it was just her remains here buried below.

The pain and sorrow of that realization crushed me again in that moment, yet once again, I lifted my hands unto God and *forced* myself to worship and praise God right there on the spot – thanking Him for her short life and again declaring my Trust in Him…

I never thought about it again, not even once that summer, as my Sister-In-Law had never mailed me the pictures from that day…

Early on after the loss of Rachel, life was so hard. Our house was so empty… without our only child. My wife's arms indeed ached for her baby…

When Christmas season came around, it was like the grief that was starting to lift - came back in full force… The beautiful red velvet dress my wife had bought our daughter to wear on Christmas was really enhancing our sorrow. We never got the chance to have even one Christmas with Rachel Ann-Marie… We would never see her wear that beautiful dress…

At the peak of the fresh grief we were now feeling so strongly (again), Christmas Eve day had arrived. We did not even want to go to our relative's house… as was the custom of our family. We just wanted to be alone…

I had picked up the mail that day and was thumbing through it when I discovered a packet that had been sent by my Sister-In-Law. Curiously I opened the packet (having completely forgotten about the pictures she had taken that day in the summer).

It was the photography envelope with all the pictures and the negative's that she had taken the day up at the cemetery that I had buried my daughter. At first it was very troubling as I was already in a lot of pain – and this was like a fresh reminder of the most difficult day in my life…

However, I started to thumb through the pictures and as I was near the end of the small stack I suddenly saw a picture that astonished me! It was different from all of the other pictures!

Every picture taken that day was in brilliant Kodak quality, just like you would see on a postcard, having been taken outdoors in the bright June sunlight with a quality camera.

I thought that this one picture might have been some kind of double exposure or something so I pulled out the negatives... I was literally shocked to discover that this one picture was right in the middle of the slide – with perfectly clear normal pictures both above this one picture and right below it too!

I knew a lady who had owned a photo processing store, so I had her look at the negatives and she confirmed to me that this was not any type of double exposure or any kind of processing irregularity because of the perfect pictures both above this picture and below it on the negatives. It was unbelievable!! Here is that picture...

This is a rendition of what the actual negatives look like, proving to the photo expert it was not a double exposure or some kind of film processing or chemical anomaly because the Picture of His Presence was in the middle - not on the end!

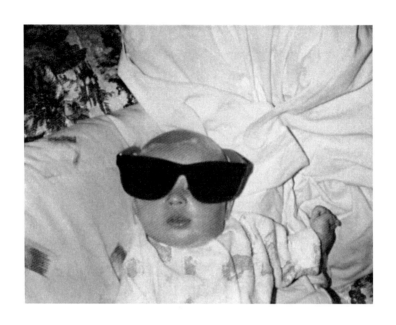

RACHEL ANN–MARIE JOHNSON

RACHEL ANN-MARIE WATCHING
BOXING WITH DAD - HONESTLY!!!

Of all the pictures taken that day, this incredible picture was the _only_ one shot where my Sister-In-Law captured me lifting lamentation worship unto the Lord! Of all the pictures taken that day – isn't it amazing the only one taken where I was in lamentation worship captured the Glory of His Presence. Can you see what happens when enter lamentation worship?

****

Again, each reader will have to judge these events on an individual basis. Was the experience holding Rachel Ann-Marie some kind of psychological manifestation based upon our deep grief and vulnerability? Was it a demonic attack and the spirit we saw was not truly our daughter and we were just simply deceived?

Was the photo we believe to literally be the Glory of God encompassing true lamentation worship or perhaps an unusual camera malfunction or faulty film?

We believe the strength of the testimony that it comes from two credible witnesses beholding the exact same experience at the exact same time (as reliable evidence) in literally seeing and holding our daughter physically and then releasing her to Heaven – all stemmed from God honoring true lamentation worship…

Is the picture, and the negatives showing perfect pictures both above and below the _only_ picture of me in the exact same function… of lamentation worship truly from the Lord?

You be the judge…

Yes, we'll gather at the river
The beautiful, the beautiful river
Gather with the saints at the river
That flows by the throne of God

THERE WILL BE A GLORIOUS RE-UNION

WITH RACHEL-ANN MARIE ONE DAY…

(THAT'S ANN-MARIE WITH A HYPHEN)

THE SONG OF HABAKKUK

"THOUGH THE FIG TREE FAILS TO BLOSSOM..."

The Prophet Habakkuk lived in a very perilous time in Israel. It was under the rule of King Jehoiakim who had led the nation back into severe idolatry and further away from the Lord God.

As a result, the nation was at the precipice of impending judgement that would soon come in the form of Israel being taken into captivity into the land of Babylon.

Habakkuk had seen the starvation of young and old, the cannibalism of children, the destruction of Solomon's Temple, and the inevitable end of his country as they knew it… It was a pretty grim time...

Habakkuk was forced to decide whether to fall into a sea of despair or rise up in bold faith and press *through* the circumstances by *choosing* to worship the Lord – (even in the midst of the storm)… He made the *choice* to *rejoice*!

Worship is a choice! The criteria for choosing to worship is not based on how *well* things are going presently in our lives, that is… if life is good – we praise, if life is bad – we sulk…

The Word of God instructs us to:

"Bless the LORD at <u>all</u> times;
His praise shall <u>continually</u> be in my mouth.
My soul shall make its boast in the LORD;
The humble shall hear of it and be glad!

Oh, *magnify* the LORD with me,
And let us *exalt* His name together.
I sought the LORD, and He heard me,
And delivered me from all my fears.
(Psalms 34:1-4)

"Rejoice in the Lord *always*. Again I
will say, rejoice!"
(Philippians 4:4)

"In *everything* give thanks (praise); for
this is the will of God in Christ Jesus
for you."
(1 Thessalonians 5:18)

But entering in to *authentic* praise and worship unto the Lord
during the time of a storm(s) in your life can be very difficult
– it is not a *given*… It *comes* by way of *choice* that *arises* up out
of *your* heart. That choice – can *only* be generated by *true* and
active faith in God at that moment…

That is a crossroad you will discover at the outset of your
storm(s) – the *choice* of faith to trust in God to bring you
through the storm(s). As you *choose* to begin to *move* into
worship *above* the trials and afflictions that have come into
your life, *your* faith begins to be released and joins into
partnership with God, empowering you to *give* Him the
burden(s) you were carrying, the burden(s) He wants to take!

The Apostle Paul must have understood the importance of
what Habakkuk penned because he quoted the prophet that
which turned out to be so revolutionary in the life of a believer

that it was the very Scripture that God used to bring forth the reformation of the church from out of the dark ages:

"…But the just shall *live* by his faith."
(Habakkuk 2:4)

Faith is the <u>critical component</u> for breakthrough in your storm(s), every bit as much as praise and worship – they work hand in hand together…

"For whatever is born of God overcomes
the world. And this is the victory that has
overcome the world—even our faith!"
(1 John 5:4)

A Testimony From The Author

At the end of the year 1999, the Lord began to give me vision for starting my own business. God gave me specific insight into building a company around a underserved, niche market that had great potential. I had the vision – but what I didn't have was the start-up capital…

My dear, sweet mother came to me unexpectedly in the latter weeks of December 1999 and said she was convinced that the vision for this company was from the Lord. She handed me four thousand dollars and said "you know that I am not rich, but I wanted to give you this seed money to help you launch your company."

The company was officially named and launched on January 1, 2000 (though we didn't legally incorporate it until January

3rd (Monday) as it was New Years Day – the first day of the new millenium… What a day to start a company!

We didn't have a building, office furniture, computers or anything (let alone a developed product ready for market…) just four thousand dollars and a lot of excitement!

As I prayed for a location (building) the Lord deeply impressed upon me a certain building in downtown Portland, Oregon. Moved by the unction of the Holy Spirit I went downtown to that small building the Lord had put on my heart… and was astonished to see a "For Rent" sign in the doorway!

I met with the property management team who oversaw the building and found out the entire second floor office area was for rent. It was 4,000 square feet in size and the landlord said it included all utilities i.e. water, garbage, electricity etc.

I asked him how much the space rented for and was flabbergasted to hear him say "it is one dollar per square foot!" At 4,000 square feet – that would be $4,000 a month, which was exactly (to the very penny) how much money I had! I mean c'mon… what are the chances of that???

I immediately starting talking to the Lord "God you can't mean you want me to rent the *full* space – if I did that, I would spend the whole $4,000 dollars I have, and all I would have to show for it is an empty space with no furniture, no computers and even more importantly – no developed product or customers to sustain this endeavor?"

There was just no way God would call me to make such a poor business decision right? I just envisioned myself going to Business & Marketing leaders of the giant metropolitan church I was a part of and telling them my business plan….

"I plan to rent this empty building and just see what the Lord will do next…" They would have thought I was crazy and suggested some kind of therapeutic counseling!

I prayed earnestly to the Lord… He answered me back…earnestly… "Yes Son, this is My plan for you." I felt sick inside and very fearful… My *real* faith was being called to account… the faith associated with real risk…

At the end of the day, I knew obedience was more importance than success, and that I needed to obey the Lord - no matter what the outcome would be… The real test would be talking to my wife… Again, I was utterly amazed when my wife said "This is God and we must follow His instruction and leave the outcome to Him!" She had more faith than me, but I eventually sucked it up and postured my heart to faith.

I went and met with the landlord and said we wanted the building. I had stirred my faith all the way up to take this $4,000 "leap" of faith.

What my faith was **not** ready for was this… The landlord said "that is excellent, I will have the papers all drawn up for the monthly lease with the owner of this building – and I think we can get the owner to drop his 60 month required commitment on the property down to perhaps a 36 month lease – but since you are a new start-up company, I know he will definitely require a *personal guarantee* from you!"

Whoah, wait a minute… A personal guarantee?? That is like signing a loan with a bank! That would place my home and car and other personal property as *collateral* against the commitment… What if this company doesn't take? I would lose my home, car and everything else… I did not like where this is going… This was <u>uncomfortable</u> faith… Sure, I had worked up faith for the $4,000 (finally), but a 36 month lease? **<u>Now</u>** how sure are you that you have "heard from God?"

Again I figured the real acid test would be approaching my wife about the matter. Women are designed by God to be security based. I shared with my wife the whole situation (or should I call it a faith crisis)? Once again I was totally and utterly amazed at my wife – so full of faith and confident that God was in this - that she was willing to risk *all* of her security in our home and property up against God's character! (Well when you put it like that…)

But still, I wish I had been as optimistic as my wife… I tried to start **<u>bargaining</u>** with God over the matter… "God can't we just see if they will rent us the first 500 square feet inside the space for 6 months so we can get on our feet, develop our product and start generating some revenue?" As you can imagine, that wasn't the Lord's plan, and He let me know it… clearly…

But when storms hit our lives, we often default to try and **<u>bargain</u>** with God. "God if you heal her I will serve you for the rest of my life…" or "God if you get me through this, I will never do this again…" etc. There is a huge challenge to our faith in these moments where we must come to the place where we *choose* to totally relinguish the situation into the hands of God – *unconditionally*… Through faith we must learn to fully *choose* to trust Him in the situation – and the final outcome – to His will and purpose – even if it doesn't match our expectation and hope in the matter… God *always* knows best!

This is a very hard lesson in life, but absolutely the wisest thing you can do. God is Faithful! God is Trustworthy! The fact of the matter is that if you *knew everything* that God *knew* concerning your situation, you too would agree with God's decisions. God is perfect! His decision and judgements are righteous! God is Love! He has *proven* Himself worthy of our complete trust! But His plans take into account the long range outcome of a matter – not just the momentary crisis itself…

I went back and signed a 36 month lease. I entered into a place of faith that I had never been to before… So now I have this beautiful empty space – all carpet. All my seed money gone. The Lord had put in my heart to establish multi-use functions for the space, so it could be used as a place for prayer in the evenings. I partnered with some prayer ministry friends who oversaw a city-wide prayer ministry.

Within a couple weeks my adversary the devil began to roar against me (of course…), attempting to strike *fear* in me. "You have a $4,000 rent payment due within 2 weeks – where are you going to get that kind of money – you don't even have a product, let alone a single paying customer." I have to admit, his attack against me was intimidating… I didn't know how that looming debt was going to be paid – and I was legally on the hook…

As it came down to just days before the rent was due, the enemy was attacking me now in full force, but I was trying hard to walk in faith and trust – (even with a growing lump of fear in my throat)… But I was determined to _stay_ in faith no matter what!

As I was driving in a car with the prayer leaders who were setting up the space to use for prayer meetings in the evenings, I begin telling them about the vision for this company that the Lord had put within my heart. Once they understood the great potential of this niche market and that I would be the first to bring much needed and desirable products to this market, they were amazed! They said "Wow, this really does has huge potential – have you ever considered taking in investors?" (Why that thought had never crossed my mind I don't know), but I told them no I hadn't.

To my utter amazement, they said "We would be glad to put in $50,000 dollars - if you are open to the idea?" Open to it??? Are you kidding me? Within the next couple of days they placed $50,000 in the company (they had been long term entrepreneurs in another very successful business that spanned across America, and provided valuable business saavy and leadership to help build a solid foundation for this new and promising business.

The rent was now paid, we bought office furniture, computer equipment etc. How sweet… I'm just a man of faith, what can I say?? (ha ha). God was moving!

What I really needed was a graphic designer and a computer programmer to help develop the niche product I knew would sell. I ended up finding both (who were a couple) just as they were graduating from Oregon State University. They were amazing… they totally understood the vision (and potential) of the company – and came on-board full-time…

Still in the early months of developing our product(s), some friends of our new investor's came to me after hearing about the fantastic opportunity this company was positioning itself for. They asked if they could invest $180,000 dollars! God was truly blessing the work… and our faith *in* Him!

These newest investors placed $90,000 into the company right then and agreed to put the other $90,000 in - later in the summer after we got up and rolling…

I had been in printing most of my life and was currently employed as a print salesman during all of this. I would work selling printing all morning for my present company, and then in the afternoon I would go over to the *new* company and work on developing and building it out.

Everything was looking good (for awhile…) In a few months down the road, we were putting the finishing touches on our newly developed product line and couldn't wait to begin marketing it. (As of yet we still had not even one customer).

Then a series of events began to unfold. Before I knew it, I was standing at my "Red Sea" (again). My employer called me one day and said "I know you are working on starting a new company – and I am all for entrepreneur endeavors, but your sales are falling here significantly and you need to make a *choice* – this job or that one!" I knew which one I must *choose*.

I told my boss "I really want to thank you for the opportunity you have given me, but I know God has entrusted this company to me so I must follow it out. I want to honor you and so I am willing to stay on with you for 30-60 days and turn over all of my customer's to whoever you hire to take my place." I was shell shocked when he said to me "No, I don't think you have to do that, as a matter of fact – you don't even need to come back to this place, I will have your assistant clean out your desk." Suddenly my <u>only</u> income was *clipped*.

I was stunned by the news. For the first time in my life I realized I was fully on my own now, with our own company…. A company that didn't even have a completely developed product yet… A company that didn't have a single paying customer yet… A company that has not made <u>*any*</u> money yet… A company with a payroll now of three… The two college grads I had hired… and *now* myself…

I realized I was going to have to start drawing a very minimal income from the company from the *dwindling* investment money still remaining in our account. I also understood that the last $90,000 our most recent investor had promised to put in later that summer was going to be needed juch sooner…

I called him up to let him know we could really use the money soon and once again, I was stunned by the news that he had tried to withdraw those funds from a special retirement account and found out he would be penalized by almost 50% if he did, so he let me know that he was not going to be able to put any more money into the business…

My world began to cave in very fast… The building rent was due, and to make matters worse – payroll was due for the first two week pay period in June of the year 2000. Our bank account was worse than I had imagined…. We did not even have enough money for payroll. I had to call in the employees and tell them "I know you are expecting to get paid today, but I am sorry to tell you – we do not have any money to pay you." The discouragement was painful… for everybody…

Ou product became finally ready for market right about then then but we had no money to launch a marketing campaign, and as a result we found ourselves in a Catch 22 situation. The next two week pay period passed quickly and *again* I had to call in the employees (feeling sick inside) "I know you are expecting to get paid today, but I am sorry to tell you – we do not have any money to pay you." Their dissappointment was obviously noticeable…

By now bills were piling up both at work and at my home. Mid-July came like a freight train - so fast and with no relief… Once again I had to call in the employees "I know you are expecting to get paid today, but we do not have any money to pay you." I was not expecting them to stay – but they did…

By now August had arrived and this storm had become excruciating… I owed several months building rent, two months payroll to the emplyees, and two months on my own home mortgage and personal bills. All in all, I had $70,000 in immediate bills due at work and $11,000 immediately due at home. I was starting to already get the first letters with language like possible eviction at the building, possible foreclosure at home, disconnection of basic utility services etc.

Once again, I had to call in the employees "I know you are expecting to get paid today, but I am sorry to tell you – we do not have any money to pay you." This could not go on…

I felt so depressed. Now we finally had our amazing product ready to market - and not a dime to use to tell people about it… I was _under_ the worst stress I had ever been in my life… I woke up with it, I carried it all day and I went to bed with it… tossing and turning…

I knew it was a matter of weeks before I would be asked to vacate the building and that the employees (who had not been paid for 2 ½ months) were ready to walk. I was doing my best to remain cool under fire… I knew even then about **praise** in the midst of the storm. My wife and I had taken our huge pile of bills (they completely covered the dining room table), and we built an altar with them – and praised the Lord over them, even danced before the Lord around them praising His name and His faithfullness. We choose to worship God in the midst of the storm in the Spirit – even though our souls felt weak and anguished. As we entered praise, (as fragile as we were) the Lord clothed us in a beautiful garment of praise for the spirit of heaviness… We were determined to trust God!

With no relief yet in sight, _again_ I had to call in the employees "I know you are expecting to get paid today, but I am sorry to tell you – we do not have any money to pay you." This time though they said "Look we truly believe in the vision of this company – but we have bills too – and unless something breaks in the next few weeks we are going to have to leave the company, so we are giving you our two week notice." I will never forget that Friday, my hope _felt_ crushed.

And who shows up at this most opportune time? My adversary, the devil… taunting me. "Well you just had to try to big the big man of faith didn't you??? This company is going down and there is nothing you can do about it. Where are you going to get nearly $100,000 in the next week??? The company is gone, your home and car are gone, your going to be sued, and your wife will most likely leave you."

The gravity of the circumstances broke my *already* broken heart into even smaller pieces… I drove home that day having to face the prospect that "Yes, from all appearances, it does *look* like this company is going down – but the one thing… the one thing I *do* have in the middle of this devastation is the <u>fact</u> that even though we are most likely going down like the Titanic, I will go down *knowing* that I was **<u>obedient</u>** to what the Lord called me to do – no matter what the outcome." My heart was resolute on that matter.

All during this times the heavens were like brass and I had not been hearing the sweet Voice of the Lord as I was accustomed to. I woke up that Saturday morning with such a heavy burden... I was hurt and discouraged… But as I prayed and cried out to the Lord, suddenly His Presence filled the room, (something I had not felt for months…). Then I heard the Lord speak to me "Son, do you think I would entrust such a company to you with this kind of potential and **<u>not</u>** require you to rise up each business morning and seek My counsel and the leading of the Holy Spirit? Do you think I would just let you make decisions that seem *right* in your eyes? I am calling you to rise up Monday morning and be on the job early enough to start each day with prayer and praise."

His voice was like finding an oasis in the desert. It was the first gleam of hope I had felt in the longest time… Monday morning, you know where I was… In the building before work, walking through each room of the business praying and praising God!! I didn't know *what* would happen but I somehow *knew* I was on the right track… prayer and praise – in the midst of the storm!

Two hours later – <u>I am not kidding</u> – two hours later I received a phone call from a man who said it was urgent that he and his partner meet with me asap. I arranged for them to come down to my building that very afternoon…

It turns out that the one guy was a stock broker, the other an insurance man. They both had the same idea as I had for this niche market. They had gone as far as creating an actual Corporation, and hired top securities lawyers from the Silicon Valley in California. Their plan was to do a Regulation "A" stcok offering for people to buy in to the business. It would raise 5 million dollars…

The only thing they didn't have – was an actual brick and mortar building and product (which I had). I listened to them with great interest (but also fearing the punchline…)

I was shocked (funny how that happens) when they said "We propose a merger of our two companies into one. You would be the President/CEO of the *new* company. You would have *sole* discretion of appointing your new Board of Directors. We would not require even a single Board seat, and we are **not** asking for employment for ourselves – we are already career men. The *only* thing we are asking is that in the newly formed company, you issue each one of us one million shares of Treasury Stock. If you are willing to do this, we can give you a check today for $200,000. I told them I would pray about it.. (just kidding….)

At that moment, I am sure I knew what Jesus must have felt like when the Angels came and fed Him and ministered unto Him just after His 40 day fast in the Judean wilderness!! I was speechless. The importance of prayer and praise in the midst of the storm became more real to me than most people will ever know – even when the battle is raging so fiercely that your heart is melting like wax… *Sing* into your storm!

The rest is history my friend… We went on to build up a powerful company. Today we are the largest provider of communications systems to Police and Firefighter Departments all across America. We are in over 1,100 cities!! We have an outstanding team of web developers, designers and software engineers. We provide communications and software programming to the Social Security Adminsitration all over America, the Department of the Treasury and even the Secret Service! It has truly a dream come true!

All of this was made possible through learning (by excruciating experience and practice), the power that can be relased in prayer and praise through the storms that come into your life. I have learned the most powerful lesson that one can know (by experience) about the faithfulness and the trustworthiness of God!

Whatever storm(s) you might find yourself in right now – don't give up!! Spend your energy on prayer and praise *instead* of buring it up on *worry, fear, doubt* or *anxiety*. The breakthrough may **not** happen overnight – but *take* heart… the Lord will deliver you!! You are not guaranteed *your* desired outcome – but you can be guaranteed His!! Relinquish the final outcome to God – He has the best plans for you. Perservere!

Don' take matters into your *own* hands… (and strength), put *everything* in His capable hands… Your God is able, faithful, compassionate and full of wisdom and power to bring about the fullest completion of His marvellous plan!

"For I know the thoughts that I think
toward _you_, says the LORD, thoughts of
peace and not of evil, to give _you_ a **future**
and a **hope**. Then _you_ will call upon Me
and go and pray to Me, and I <u>will</u> listen
to _you_. And _you_ will seek Me and find Me,
when _you_ search for Me with **all** _your_ heart."
(Jeremiah 29:11-13)

You must press through to the other side! Don't give up! You have got to see what the Lord has in all this. Every trial has Divine Purpose!! I strongly suggest reading another book by Paul E. Billheimer called "Don't Wast Your Sorrows." It will give you incredible insight as what God can do in the midst of every storm you will ever face in this life – because God actually authorizes them to happen! (with purpose…)

Habakkuk 3:17-19

THE SONGS OF DELIVERANCE

"SONGS IN THE NIGHT"

To everything there is a *season*,
a time for every *purpose* under heaven:

A time to be born, and a time to die;
A time to plant, and a time to pluck *what is* planted;
A time to kill, and a time to heal;
A time to break down, and a time to build up;
A time to weep, and a time to laugh;
A time to mourn, and a time to dance;
A time to cast away stones, and a time to gather stones;
A time to embrace, and a time to refrain from embracing;
A time to gain, and a time to lose;
A time to keep, and a time to throw away;
A time to tear, and a time to sew;
A time to keep silence, and a time to speak;
A time to love, and a time to hate;
A time of war, and a time of peace…
(Ecclesiastes 3:1-8)

In our journey through this life we all come to know good *times* and bad *times*, and both joy and sorrow. One minute we can feel like we are on top of the mountain and the next minute we can find ourselves cascade down, and walking through the valley of the shadow of death.

One of the most valuable lessons that <u>you</u> will ever learn in this life is the ability to *see beyond* the circumstances of the hardships that you will inevitably encounter… The focal point we must press towards is to gain a heavenly perspective (focus) upon God *and* His purposes (Will) for our life. The greatest demonstration of this difficult (but precious truth), is found in the Bible where we read:

"…who for the *joy* that was set before Him
endured the cross, despising the shame, and
has sat down at the right hand of the throne of God."
(Hebrews 12:2)

Of course we all know this Scripture, but we tend to reconcile its meaning in our minds to the rationale that "of course, but that was Jesus, the strong and powerful Son of God."

But yet in the Garden of Gethsemane, Jesus *knowing* that He is at the threshold of an impending, agonizing and painful death upon the cross, became:

"…and He began to be *sorrowful* and
deeply distressed. Then He said to them,
My soul is exceedingly *sorrowful*, even
to death… He went a little farther and
fell on His face, and prayed, saying,
O My Father, if it is possible, let this cup
pass from Me; nevertheless, not as I will,
but as You *will*."
(Matthew 26:37-39)

"…And being in *agony*, He prayed more
earnestly. Then His sweat became like great
drops of blood falling down to the ground."
(Luke 22:44)

It almost sounds like a contradiction in that all of these Scriptures we see surrounding the events and circumstances leading up to the cross… How is it possible to have *joy* when you are *sorrowful, deeply distressed* or in *agony*? How?

Keeping perspective!! Even in the midst of a dichotomy... What is a dichotomy? The Merriam Webster dictionary says:

"It is a division into two especially *mutual* but *contradictory* groups or entities; i.e. the *dichotomy* between theory and practice; *also*: the process or practice of making such a division."

In other words, two things (seemingly diametrically opposed to each other), occurring from the same situation (person). Jesus said that "His <u>soul</u> was *sorrowful* – His <u>physical</u> and <u>emotional</u> well-being were *deeply distressed* and in *agony*. Yet in that garden, His spirit, **kept perspective** of God and His purposes and Jesus spirit <u>over-ruled</u> His body and soul unto remaining resolute concerning the Will of God! Was it easy? **No**! Was it painful? **Yes**! Did He do it? **Yes**! It's the reason you are in the Kingdom of God today!

We too must learn this indispensable truth:

"He who is slow to anger is better than
the mighty, and he who *<u>rules</u>* his spirit is
better than he who captures a fortified city!"
(Proverbs 16:32)

Keeping perspective… Can it be done? The Bible says yes:

"Consider (keep perspective) it *pure joy*,
my brothers and sisters, <u>whenever</u> you
face trials of many kinds, because you
know that the testing of your faith produces
perseverance. Let perseverance finish its
work so that you may be mature and
complete, not lacking anything."
(James 1:2-4)

"In this you greatly *rejoice*, though now for
a little while, if need be, you have been
grieved by various trials, that the genuineness
of your faith, being much more precious than
gold that perishes, though it is tested by fire,
may be found to praise, honor, and glory at
the revelation of Jesus Christ."
(1 Peter 1:6, 7)

At different points in our life-long walk with God we will encounter what the saints of old referred to as **"the dark night of the soul"**. To everything there is a season… A time for every purpose under Heaven. When those times (seasons) come, learning to **keep perspective**, as Christ did, will be the single most difficult, yet most crucial and important thing you can do!

God never loses control, and He will never leave you! He is with you in the midst of every storm! Look for Jesus standing in the midst of your tempest saying (as He did to His disciples that day on the Sea of Galilee) "Don't be afraid, IAM!"

 As a matter of fact, according to the Word of God:

"You shall have a song in the night
when a holy feast is kept, and gladness
of heart as when one marches in procession
with a flute to go to the temple on the
mountain of the Lord, to the Rock of Israel."
(Isaiah 30:29)

"Where *is* God my Maker, who
gives songs in the night…"
(Job 35:10)

"Deep calls unto deep at the noise of Your
waterfalls; all Your waves and billows have
gone over me. The LORD <u>will</u> command His
loving-kindness in the daytime, and in the
night His **song** *shall be* with me—
a prayer to the God of my life."
(Psalms 42: 7, 8)

"I call to remembrance my *song* in the night;
I meditate within my heart, and my spirit
makes diligent search."
(Psalms 77:6)

Friend you may be going through the dark night of the soul
right now… A time of great sorrow, distress, doubt, hurt,
confusion, sickness or great need. As overwhelming as it is to
you – God is with you right now! His heart is tender towards
you. He promises you (personally):

"No temptation (trial or hardship) has
overtaken you except such as is common
to man; but God is *faithful,* who will *not*
allow you to be tempted beyond what you
are able, but with the temptation will also
make the way of escape, that you may be
able to bear it."
(1 Corinthians 10:13)

You have a Great High Priest who has been through it too!

"For we have not a high priest which
cannot be touched with the feeling
(compassion) of our infirmities; but
was in all points tempted like *us,*

yet without sin."
(Hebrews 4:15)

God will **make a way** for you!! It may not happen instantly, God is not a microwave God – but He is *faithful*! Let your faith *rest* upon His Word. Let Him prove it! Position your heart in praise and worship. Enter the *rest* He has prepared for you!

"Let us labor therefore to enter into
that rest, lest any man fall after the
same example of unbelief."
(Hebrews 4:11)

In the dark of the night – lift up voice! He is not just a daytime God – but the God of your night season(s) too!! He will give you a *song* that can be released into your heart *through* faith as you *choose* to *place* your trust in the Lord.

The Lord will give you the *song of the nightingale…* The nightingale songbird is among a rare species whose sweet *song* is only heard in the still of the night. Almost all other songbirds lift up their song in and around the breaking of dawn. Why not *choose* to lift up your song unto the Lord– just like the nightingale… lift up a song in the night!

Paul and Silas were severely beaten by the local authorities in Philippi and then locked into an extra secure, inner jail cell and then on top of that, their feet were put into stocks… Yet even at midnight, the other prisoners could hear them *singing* **joyfully** – *songs in the night*!

"Then the multitude rose up together
against them; and the magistrates tore
off their clothes and commanded them
to be beaten with rods. And when they
had laid many stripes on them, they threw

them into prison, commanding the jailer to
keep them securely. Having received such
a charge, he put them into the inner prison
and fastened their feet in the stocks.

But at midnight Paul and Silas were praying
and *singing* hymns to God, and the prisoners
were listening to them... Suddenly there was
a great earthquake, so that the foundations of
the prison were shaken; and immediately all
the doors were opened and everyone's chains
were loosed."
(Acts 16:22-26)

Your *song in the night* can move Heaven too! The Lord will
surround you with songs of **deliverance**… But will *you* receive
them into *your* heart?

"You are *my* hiding place; You shall
preserve me (watch over, guard, keep,
defend) from trouble; You shall surround
me with *songs of deliverance*."
(Psalms 32:7)

"I love the LORD, because He has heard
my voice (*song*) and my supplications (*prayer*).
Because He has inclined His ear to me,
Therefore I will call upon Him as long as I live.
The pains of death surrounded me,
And the pangs of Sheol laid hold of me;
I found trouble and sorrow.
Then I called upon the name of the LORD:
O LORD, I implore You, deliver my soul!

Gracious *is* the LORD, and righteous;
Yes, our God *is* merciful.

The LORD preserves the simple;
I was brought low, and He saved me.
Return to your *rest*, O my soul,
For the LORD has dealt bountifully with you.

For You have delivered my soul from death,
My eyes from tears,
And my feet from falling."
(Psalms 116:1-8)

The transition from a place of turmoil and anxiety in the midst of your storm(s) over to God is not an easy one…. We can't just flip a switch and it's done. It **has** to come from rendering a heart decision to *choose* to incline *your* heart and *your* mind unto the Lord and begin to release true trust unto Him, fully relinquishing the storm(s) that have assailing *you* to His care. It is an act of *your* faith in action. Give God *your* storm(s)!

"Blessed *be* the LORD, because He has
heard the voice of my supplications!
The LORD is my strength and my shield;
my heart trusted in Him, and I am *helped*;
therefore my heart greatly rejoices, and
with my *song* I will praise Him."
(Psalms 28:6, 7)

Your dark night (season) will eventually pass. The promises of the Lord are sure… How you navigate the storm(s) in *your* life is a *matter of the heart*… God is worthy of your trust, no matter how difficult *your* situation! Remember - He is *Baal Perazim*, the God of *your* breakthrough! He is *your* waymaker!

Encountering severe storm(s) in our life continually beg the question in our minds… why? The natural mind will just by default, will automatically develop a variety of explanations i.e. God is punishing me, the devil is oppressing me, it's just my bad luck etc.

We can exert an enormous amount of energy trying to ascertain answers. The reality in every storm, is that the actual cause *could* be any number of reasons – but _why_ is not the right question! The right question is _what_? What is this unto?

It's learning to _inquire_ of the Lord of what possible purpose could there be in this storm(s) that I can learn and grow from. (Regardless of the **_cause_**… what is the **_purpose_**?)

There is Divine Opportunity to actually grow and develop into ever-increasing maturity in Christ through *every* storm we will ever encounter.

Ask yourself… Can the Fruit of the Spirit be ripened (sweetened) through this storm… Can my character be more developed in Christ… Can my faith be strengthened to trust the Lord more and more… Can a powerful testimony come forth that will encourage and strengthen others as they face similar storms?

We constantly miss heavenly benefit through many storms in our life because we _chose_ not to engage **heaven's perspective** in the matter. Every storm is an *opportunity* to bear fruit, grow spiritually, and worship Christ from a deeper, intimate place!

Don't *waste* your sorrows! With the *right perspective* you can maximize each difficult storm in _your_ life and actually extract from it exceedingly precious and valuable things!

Black clouds can have silver linings! I heard Ray Hughes once say that "Sometimes the purest cleansing rain falls from the darkest black clouds…"

God will encompass thee about! He will surround you with *songs of deliverance*! If you only knew the full story behind many of the great hymns that you have sang for years… Many were written in the midst of unspeakable tragedy, pain, sorrow and suffering. Here is just one incredible example:

Annie Johnson Flint (1866-1932) lost both parents before she was six years of age. She was adopted, but while still in her teen years she became afflicted with arthritis and unable to walk. Though she aspired to become a composer and concert pianist, her illness deprived her of that ability so she resorted to writing poetry.

In her later life, being unable to even open her hands, she wrote many of her poems on a typewriter – using her knuckles. From her own deep affliction, she wrote one of the most beautiful and awe-inspiring hymns ever heard:

HE GIVETH MORE GRACE

He giveth more Grace, as our burdens grow greater,
He sendeth more Strength as our labors increase,
To added affliction, He addeth His Mercy,
To multiplied trials, He multiplies Peace.

When we have exhausted our store of endurance,
When our strength has failed, ere the day half-done,
When we reach the end of our hoarded resources,
Our Father's full giving – has only begun…

His Love has no limits, His Grace has no measure,
His Power, no boundary – known unto man,
For out of His infinite Riches in Jesus,
He giveth, and giveth, and giveth again…

The author based her words on three precious promises from the Word of God:

1) "He giveth more Grace…" (James 4:6)
2) "He increaseth strength" (Isaiah 40:29)
3) "Mercy, Peace, and Love be multiplied" (Jude 2)

Oh that we would discover His precious Presence in the midst of our storm(s)! That we would press into Jesus, casting all of our burden(s) upon Him, and let Him flood our hearts with *songs in the night – songs* of deep worship, praise, and trust in Him… *songs* of faith, *songs* of deliverance – arising from a heart with gaining confidence:

"Lo, I am with thee – unto the end
of the world. Amen."
(Matthew 28:20)

I WILL NEVER LEAVE YOU

NOR FORSAKE YOU!!

HEBREWS 13:5

THE SONG OF THE BARREN

"SING INTO YOUR BARRENNESS"

The opening of the Book of Samuel tells of the incredible story of Hannah – a barren woman. To be barren in Hannah's time was as a curse in society – for you were looked down upon with disdain, bearing the reproach of having some type of flaw in character…

To make matters worse for Hannah, her husband Elkanah had another wife Peninnah (who had given him children). Peninnah continually vexed Hannah about her barrenness:

"…and her rival (Peninnah) also provoked
her severely, to make her miserable…"
(1 Samuel 1:6)

"So it was, year by year, when she went up
to the house of the LORD, that she (Peninnah)
provoked her; therefore she wept and did not eat."
(1 Samuel 1:7)

"And she was in bitterness of soul, and prayed to
the LORD and wept in anguish."
(1 Samuel 1:10)

Hannah did not have a fertility problem…

"…the LORD had closed her womb."
(1 Samuel 1:5)

In the midst of her storm, Hannah made a vow to the Lord. She told Him that if He would give her a male child, that she would dedicate him unto lifelong service in the House of God.

"And it happened, as she continued praying before the LORD, that Eli watched her mouth. Now Hannah *spoke* in her heart (connotes singing/consoling within her heart…); only her lips moved, but her voice was not heard. Therefore Eli thought she was drunk. So Eli said to her, how long will you be drunk? Put your wine away from you!

But Hannah answered and said, No, my lord, I am a woman of sorrowful spirit. I have drunk neither wine nor intoxicating drink, but have poured out my soul (lamentation worship) before the LORD. Do not consider your maidservant a wicked woman, for out of the abundance of my complaint and grief I have spoken until now." (1 Samuel 1:12-16)

"Then they rose early in the morning and *worshiped* before the LORD, and returned and came to their house at Ramah. And Elkanah *knew* Hannah his wife, and the LORD *remembered* her… So it came to pass in the process of time that Hannah conceived and bore a son, Samuel, saying, because I have asked for him from the LORD." (1 Samuel 1:19, 20)

Through her dark night of the soul, and her anguish, the Lord brought her to the place of desperation and consecration. But from her womb would come destiny for Israel… a Prophet of prophets would one day anoint and confirm a king in Israel (David) upon whose throne - God would bring forth His Son and establish an everlasting Throne!

Through and beyond seasons of barrenness, God has brought forth many of the greatest servants of God ever found throughout the entire Bible! Isaac, Israel, Samson, Samuel & John the Baptist…were all born to women who had once been barren…

The Word of God admonishes those in barrenness to **_sing_**! And not only to _sing_, but to _sing_ directly into the very barrenness itself! This is _singing into your storm_! With faith!!!

"_Sing_, O barren, you who have not borne!
Break forth into _singing_, and cry aloud, you
who have not labored with child! For more
are the children of the desolate than the
children of the married woman, says the LORD."
(Isaiah 54:1)

What? You can't be serious? Can you imagine a barren woman in ancient Israel being told to just _sing into_ her barrenness? One who is already ridiculed by others, feeling shame and probably feeling abandoned by God? Sometimes even being rejected by their own husband's for not being able to bear children?

Singing into your barrenness is an act of deep worship – and an act of faith. It is **not** a _guarantee_ you will become pregnant… But is releases to the Lord a heart that becomes _bonded_ to His through your despaired and broken heart.

"He _heals_ the brokenhearted, and
binds up their wounds."
(Psalms 147:3)

"The LORD *is* near to those who have a
broken heart, and saves such as have a
contrite spirit."
(Psalms 34:18)

It establishes a posture of heart unto the Lord whereupon He
can possess the very depths of your being… of your heart!

"Whom have I in Heaven but You?
And there is nothing upon earth that
I desire besides You… My flesh and
my heart fail; but God is the strength
of my heart and my portion forever."
(Psalms 73:25-26)

Perhaps your barrenness might not be in the inability to bear
children. You might be experiencing a time or season in life
where you're well has run dry, where ministry aspirations
have not reached the height of the vision or has left you with
a severe lack of productivity from all of your labors… feelings
of emptiness, deprivation, lack of fulfillment, or harvest.

The Word of God instructs us to *sing* into those very areas of
barrenness! *Sing* of God's Love, mercy, faithfulness, kindness,
goodness, provision etc. _Choose_ to worship God right into the
very area of your barrenness. *Sing* His promises back to Him!

"But You are holy, _enthroned_ in
the praises of Israel."
(Psalms 22:3)

You can **enthrone** the Living God right into the midst of the
barrenness in your life. By so doing, you are inviting the great
IAM – to come and dwell in the midst of your dry and barren
land (situation)… He is *more than enough* in every instance!

But we must always remember that praise does not guarantee our *preferred* outcome – (to the exact specifications we have requested of God through our song or intercessory worship). We *still* must exert complete trust in the all-knowing, all-powerful God who is always for our highest good... In order to trust God fully in a situation (storm), you must be steadfast in heart to receive the outcome of His discretion.

We must learn to be *content* with the portion He gives, and the final outcome He brings... That is faith in its purest form – complete trust dependency upon the Lord – fully leaning (*resting*) on His *goodness, wisdom and power*!

We all go through times or seasons in our walk with God where our *"well"* seems to have dried up. We don't feel the anointing in operation as we have in other seasons, the heavens seem like brass to us (closed), and even His voice seems hard to hear...

Lifting **praise** to God can open up our innermost being and cause waters to flow (again...).

Nearing the end of the journey in the wilderness, the children of Israel came to a place of need of water. The Lord instructed Moses to gather the people, for the Lord was about to give them water - that He promised to give them. What was there job? To *sing into their storm*!

Then Israel sang this song:

Spring up, O well!
All of you *sing* to (into) it!"
(Numbers 21:17)

Do you need *living water* to flow again? There is a well that runs deep within you! It might have *seemingly* gone dry for any number of reasons – but that is not the issue. Instead of focusing on the problem, why not focus on the solution?

Why not start re-digging your well with praise and worship and don't stop! **_Sing_** into your well! High Praise will prime the pump – and before you know it… your dry ground will soon experience – _living water!_"

Sing to the Lord right down into the very midst of your well! **_Sing_** to the Lord of the many past times His faithfulness has shown up for you! **_Sing_** with faith and expectation of the Lord to move within your present circumstances. **_Sing_** unto the Lord "SPRING UP O WELL"!

Has not the Lord promised?

Is not the Word of the Lord sure?

"God _is_ not a man, that He should lie,
nor a son of man, that He should repent.
Has He said, and will He not do?
(Numbers 23:19)

"If _anyone_ thirsts, let him come to Me
and drink. He who **_believes_** in Me, as
the Scripture has said, out of his heart
will flow rivers of living water."
(John 7:38)

Work on your waterways… Dig. Dig. Dig through praise! Set apart _daily_ times of dedicated worship unto the Lord. Go back through all of your worship mp3's, cd's (and cassettes!!) and compile a stack of the deepest, most intimate and meaningful worship songs you have ever flowed with God from in the past. You will tap into the river of God – don't give up! Press!

Continuous **praise** changes everything. It is your *life-spring* and your *well-spring*! **Praise** must be a priority. Everything else will begin to flow eventually. Stay immersed in Christ!

As you are faithful to do this *daily*, the Lord will cause the water of His Spirit to begin to flow and literally soften potential areas of hard ground in your heart. Many times when the Lord brings you into a season of dryness – He is after something in the long run and is wanting to expose areas of hardness of heart – areas that have become (or have always been) unfruitful, unproductive, barren!

His long term objective is *always* to cultivate those areas so that He can begin to prepare good soil in your heart where He can plant what He desires in those areas. It takes *co-operation* from us in working with Him to accomplish this. Extended times of praise…will greatly help this process along.

As you begin to do business with God afresh in these areas, **sing** into the midst of His work in your heart. One of my favorite songs in this process is:

Soften My Heart

Soften my heart with oil
Open my eyes to see
Fill me with understanding
Soften my heart to receive

I want all that You have for me, Jesus
All that You have for me
Open my understanding
Soften my heart to receive
I want all that You have for me

Don't let my heart to be fallen
Don't let my heart be hard
Water me with Your Spirit
Soften the ground of my heart

I want all that You have for me, Jesus
All that You have for me
Open my understanding
Soften my heart to receive
I want all that You have for me

In my own life during times of dryness and barrenness that simple song began to break up the large clods of hardness in my heart, enabling me to come into deeper fellowship with Christ through the Holy Spirit. It helped me to fan back into flame a fire that many times was down to just a pilot light! It helped me to move into a season where I became willing to let God do some gardening in my life… The Lord can use seasons of barrenness to get our attention…

God is clear in His word.

"You did not choose Me, but I chose *you*
and appointed *you* that you should go and
bear *fruit*, and that your fruit should *remain*…"
(John 15:16)

"By this My Father is glorified, that *you* bear
 much *fruit*; so *you* will be My disciples.
(John 15:8)

"I am the true vine, and My Father is the
vinedresser. Every branch in Me that does
not bear *fruit* He takes away; and every branch
that bears fruit He *prunes*, that it may bear more
fruit. You are already clean because of the word

which I have spoken to you. Abide in Me, and I in you. As the branch cannot bear *fruit* of itself, unless it abides in the vine, neither can <u>you</u>, unless you abide in Me."
(John 15:1-4)

The Lord wants to do a mighty work in <u>your</u> areas of barrenness so that it becomes rich, fertile land that is choice for the planting of the Lord!

Continuous praise will both start (and keep) the River flowing from your inner-most being and help to irrigate the fields of your heart.

By *co-operating* with the Lord in this process, during your season of barrenness, your will be letting God prepare to plant in you – **His field of dreams**! It all starts with *singing* into your barrenness!

IT'S TIME TO RE-DIG YOUR WELL!!

THE SONG OF DEBORAH

"AWAKE, AWAKE DEBORAH!"

Deborah like Miriam, was a prophetess… Just one of a few actually mentioned in the Old Testament history of Israel. In the times of Deborah, Israel had fallen into deep sin and idolatry and there was great oppression in the land. Israel had been under this continual attack and aggression for over 20 years straight, at the hands of King Jabin, a wicked and cruel Canaanite King, and his merciless Army Commander, Sisera.

This endearing storm in Israel became so intense, the people were fearful of even going out to draw water from the surrounding wells because Canaanite marauders would spring forth out of hiding and rob them. After years and years of relentless attacks, the people of Israel did what they should have done all along –

"And the children of Israel cried
out to the Lord."
(Judges 4:3)

How much oppression should you endure before you finally reach a breaking point, and a righteous indignation fuels a holy violence to arise from deep within you?

You might be in a "hurricane season" in your life right now, where powerful hurricanes are slamming into your life repeatedly, causing much damage… Physically, emotionally, spiritually, financially, relationally etc.

Or it might be that you are experiencing a prolonged storm, like a nightmare - that just won't seem to dissipate and it has rendered you weak, discouraged, depressed and bleak.

In either case, you need to begin moving Heaven on your behalf! You can actually activate (demand) your faith to arise, that will draw forth *hidden courage* from deep within you! Just determine *in your heart* to break forth into **praise** – and *choose* to fully *trust* Christ, no matter the outcome... When you fully surrender your storm to God, you set the Lord to become *your* very defense!

"My soul, wait silently for God alone,
For *my* expectation *is* from Him.
He *only* is my Rock and *my* Salvation;
He is *my* Defense;
I shall *not* be moved.
In God is *my* Salvation and *my* Glory;
The Rock of *my* strength,
And *my* Refuge, is in God.
Trust in Him at all times, *you* people;
Pour out *your* heart before Him;
God is a Refuge for us. *Selah*
(Psalms 62:5-8)

With Deborah, (as with Miriam), what ended up being a victory song that was sang *after* the battle – could have been a *song of victory* sang prophetically through faith – beforehand rather than a *song of deliverance* sang afterwards...

Although it is certainly wise and prudent to give thanks and praise to our God continually, doing so *after* the battle is won or after the breakthrough has come – requires no faith at all! *Hindsight* praise is honoring – but how much **more** by faith in the midst of the storm! You see:

"But without faith it is _impossible_ to please Him, for he who comes to God must believe that He is, and that He is a _rewarder_ of those who diligently seek Him."
(Hebrews 11:6)

We were created to worship God, for He is worthy of our praise at _all_ times… We were created for His good pleasure, the point here is that, how much more pleasure we bring Him, when we _choose_ to place all of trust in Him, I mean completely lay it on the line… especially in the midst of a raging storm?

He has declared His everlasting Love for us, His faithfulness to all generations… The children of Israel believed that God loved them enough to bring them out of Egypt, but they obviously _didn't_ believe that He loved them _enough_ to bring them fully into the Promised Land… If they had… they never would have perished in the wilderness.

"The Song of Deborah" is hallowed even today by our Jewish brothers and sisters. It is sang alongside _"The Song of Moses"_ at the Feasts… Both are glorious songs of praise that detail a mighty deliverance through the God of Abraham, Isaac and Jacob for His people.

After the great and mighty victory of war, Deborah and Barak led forth the powerful, declarative song of victory and triumph. It is even recorded in the Jewish annals of history with other songs or triumphs like David's mighty victory of Goliath. How much more _glorious_ could that victory had been with adamant faith through praise going forth in the battle first?

The purpose of this book is to *charge* the faith of each reader who may be encountering a massive storm of some kind in their lives to **not** wait until the final outcome of the battle comes before giving thanks and praise to God (as we see in the song of Deborah), but rather to harness the power of praise _now_... as a formidable weapon in the midst of _your_ storm – that kind of faith and trust overwhelms the very heart of God.

Your praise in the midst of the storm makes the strongest statement to Heaven possible… It is the declaration that you have _chosen_ to place your trust (faith) fully in Christ, (which greatly pleases God) and also moves the power of Heaven in releasing the dunamis power of the Holy Spirit as well as deploying angelic forces on your behalf. This kind of response to your storm will deepen your intimacy with God, while establishing an impacting testimony that can significantly affect and encourage others as they experience similar storm in their life! It's the win-win-win scenario (you win, God wins and others win)

Couldn't you just imagine Deborah summoning Barak (before the battle took place) and speaking to him prophetically concerning God's strategic plan to route the oppressive enemy, King Jabin once and for all? Then charging Barak to summon the tribes of Israel to gather in prophetic assembly before the Lord...

Then in that corporate gathering, Deborah begins to *sing* as a true prophetess – the prophetic heart of God and His plans for battle! In the *Song of Deborah*, she opens this incredible song with a powerful declaration of what happens when leadership stands up, and the people of God get behind what the Lord is saying and doing. The opening lines of the song of Deborah are:

"When leaders lead in Israel,
When the people willingly offer themselves,
Bless the LORD!"
(Judges 5:1, 2)

Then Deborah begins to *sing* about the faithfulness of God and His preservation of Israel in previous times – just as David did in his dark night "I will encourage myself in the Lord" (David recounting the mighty deeds and victories the Lord had brought him through… demanding his soul take note, be refreshed in God's power and faithfulness that he had experienced continually throughout his life…. Deborah sings:

"Hear, O kings! Give ear, O princes!
I, *even* I, will sing to the LORD;
I will sing praise to the LORD God of Israel.
LORD, when You went out from Seir,
When You marched from the field of Edom,
The earth trembled and the heavens poured,
The clouds also poured water;
The mountains gushed before the LORD,
This Sinai, before the LORD God of Israel."
(Judges 5:3-5)

What Deborah is *singing* about is how God moved so mightily in Israel's **past**… just as He did faithfully did for them in their battle (but again, I believe this *song* could have been sung beforehand – not just *after* the battle was over).

For God sent forth a plentiful downpour of rain from Heaven so strong that it immobilized Sisera's army and their chariots and they got stuck in the mud! As a result the enemy was routed and the victory secured!

"The kings came *and* fought,
Then the kings of Canaan fought
In Taanach, by the waters of Megiddo;
They took no spoils of silver.
They fought from the heavens;
The stars from their courses fought against Sisera.
The torrent of Kishon swept them away,
That ancient torrent, the torrent of Kishon.
O my soul, march on in strength!
Then the horses' hooves pounded,
The galloping, galloping of his steeds.

What if the prophetess Deborah had opened this *song before* the ensuing battle, preparing the people to send for praise unto their God beforehand standing there in corporate assembly? A *song* to open the Heavens before them, and call upon the Lord their God as a Mighty Man of War to arise?

"Awake, awake, Deborah!
Awake, awake, sing a song!
Arise, Barak, and lead your captives away,
O son of Abinoam!"
(Judges 5:12)
It could have been a prophetic war cry, calling the camp to a fresh faith, stirring up zeal in their hearts as they prepared for battle.

Declaring unto the Lord their confidence in Him to go before them!! With a mighty closing declaration of the power, and jealous love their God could have demonstrated to them in the midst of their praise by showing Himself strong!

"Thus let all Your enemies perish, O LORD!
But let those who love Him _be_ like the sun
When it comes out in full strength."
(Judges 5:31)

You have choice before every storm that crosses your path…

You can _sing_ into the midst of it, _sing_ about it later,
or not _sing_ (praise God) about it at all.

 May heavenly history record **_your_** praise, faith and courage!

DEBORAH & BARAK

THE SPIRITUAL SONGS

"HE PUT A NEW SONG IN MY MOUTH"

Learning to *sing* into your storm(s) is a progressive discipline that grows and matures like other fruit. It is not a mathematical equation like: singing + God = answered prayer.

Your *song* <u>must</u> be mixed with faith, be properly aligned with the Word & Will of God, and have *fusion* with the Holy Spirit. What is *fusion*?

Merriam-Webster Dictionary defines it as:

1. The *union* of atomic nuclei to form heavier nuclei resulting in the *release* of enormous quantities of energy when certain light elements unite.
2. A *merging* of diverse, distinct, or separate elements into a unified whole.
3. Popular *music* (song) combining different styles.

When storms encompass you, deep in the recesses of your heart you must make a decision… Whether you are going to *place* your trust in Christ to sustain you through the storm or end up being inundated by the circumstances or elements of the storm itself and its impact…

Please do not misunderstand me, I know your storm is very real… and perhaps *overwhelming*. You may be experiencing one of the greatest trials in your life… severe pain, loss, tragedy, abuse, depression, anxiety… the list could surely go on and on…

But the very heart of God's desire for you – is to not *succumb* to the circumstances. What does succumb mean?

Merriam-Webster Dictionary defines it as:

1. To yield to superior strength or force from an overpowering appeal or desire i.e. *"succumb* to temptation…"
2. To be brought to an end (as death) by the effect of destructive or disruptive forces.

On one-hand your storm may be the direct result of a satanic attack against you or your loved ones. It is certainly always the plan of the wicked one to try and overthrow your faith.. it has happened to many…

"…Some having rejected, concerning
the faith have suffered shipwreck."
(1 Timothy 1:19)

We have an adversary who constantly tries to discourage us, badger us, tempt us, lie to us, hinder us etc. Faith is a fight! Faith has an enemy! What did the Apostle Paul say near the end of his life?

"I have *fought* the good fight, I have
finished the race, I have **kept the faith**.
Finally, there is laid up for me the crown
of righteousness, which the Lord, the
righteous Judge, will give to me on that
Day, and not to me only but also to all
who have loved His appearing."
(2 Timothy 4:7-8)

Or perhaps your storm may be of completely different nature, having come from an unexpected event in your life like a serious illness, job loss, tragic accident, or deep wound at the hand of someone else… Whatever the source of your storm stems from – _you_ have a greater _Source_ available to you! God!

The Word of God speaks to us about lifting up a _song_ to the Lord. Throughout the Bible we see:

"…_singing_ and making melody
in _your_ heart to the Lord."
(Ephesians 5:19)

"Oh, _sing_ to the LORD a new song!
Sing to the LORD, all the earth. _Sing_
to the LORD, bless His name; proclaim
the good news of His salvation from
day to day."
(Psalms 96:1-2)

"_Sing_ to the LORD a new song, and
His praise from the ends of the earth…"
(Isaiah 42:10)

"Oh, sing to the LORD a new song! For
He has done marvelous things; His right
hand and His holy arm have gained Him
the victory. The LORD has made known
His salvation…"
(Psalms 98:1)

We see different connotations and examples of _songs_ like **psalms, hymns and spiritual songs**… Some are meant to be sung unto the Lord, some to be sung over other people to help encourage, comfort and strengthen them, and some _songs_ come by direct inspiration of the Holy Spirit whereupon the

Lord will *sing* (by His Holy Spirit) through <u>us</u> over people, situations, and yes... even storms...

Psalms

Psalms can be broken down into two different classes... *poetic* and *prophetic*. David was called the sweet Psalmist of Israel, and wrote many of the Psalms in the Bible. The title to the Book of "Psalms" (*Tehilliam*) means "songs of praise" or better said "Sacred *songs* or *poems* sung to musical accompaniment."

Psalms arise from the deepest, heartfelt condition of the heart and soul. They can extol, bless and glorify God with thanksgiving, or bear unto the Lord the depths of pain, suffering, and sorrow in lament like David describes below:

"I am weary with my groaning; all night
I make my bed swim; I drench my couch
with my tears. My eye wastes away because
of grief; it grows old because of all my enemies."
(Psalms 6:6-7)

Psalms can also be as *prayers* to the Lord:

"The prayers (Psalms) of David the
son of Jesse are ended."
(Psalms 72:20)

Psalms can also become very *prophetic* as you immerse yourself in the Spirit of the Lord through psalmic worship.
A classic example is David's stunningly accurate prophetic psalm about the crucifixion of Christ - something like a thousand years beforehand:

"I am poured out like water, and all
My bones are out of joint; My heart is
like wax; it has melted within Me. My
strength is dried up like a potsherd, and
My tongue clings to My jaws; You have
brought Me to the dust of death. For dogs
have surrounded Me; The congregation of
the wicked has enclosed Me. They pierced
My hands and My feet; I can count all My
bones. They look and stare at Me. They
divide My garments among them, And for
My clothing they cast lots.
(Psalms 22:14-18)

For our purpose here, we can gain much insight in how King David used the psalms in worship through the midst of his storms, and how we too can employ the power of psalmic praise in our darkest hours. Fifty of the recorded psalms are lamentations unto the Lord! Yet in the midst of hearts pouring out their burden unto the Lord, practically all of those psalms end with praise to the Most High God.

Here are roughly 40 lamentation psalms recorded in the Bible. We encourage you to read them and as you do – whatever portions resonate with you concerning your present situation… use the Psalms by making personal declarations, prayers and praise unto the Lord:

Psalms: 3, 4, 5, 7, 9, 10, 13, 14, 17, 22, 25, 26, 27, 28, 31, 36, 39, 40, 41, 42, 43, 52, 53, 54, 55, 56, 57, 59, 61, 64, 69, 70, 71, 77, 86, 89, 120, 139, 141, 142.

Your praying and worshipping Christ through the psalms will begin to release *your* powerful, intercessory *song* before the Throne of Grace, in a time of need. As you do, the Spirit of the Lord will begin to flood your heart.

The Spirit of the Lord will surely start to "inhabit" the praise of your heartfelt lamentation, boldness, confidence and faith that you lift up unto the Lord!

In that incredible place in the Spirit, you can literally *learn* how to begin to *sing* into your storm, declaring the faithfulness of God, the power of His Mighty Hand, the release of His healing virtue, the names (character) of God like Jehovah Raphe, the Lord *your* Healer, Jehovah Shalom, the God of *your* Peace, even to begin *singing in the Spirit* about the release of forgiveness to those who have caused such a deep wound in your life.

"…Weeping may last for night
but joy comes in the morning."
(Psalms 30:5)

Yes there will come *your* time of breakthrough and deliverance (the daybreak of Divine intervention and answered prayer).

Your will see fruit come forth from the womb of the morning!

The Lord is so caring and compassionate towards us that He implores us to:

"Cast all of your cares upon Him,
for He cares for _you_ – always!
(1 Peter 5:7)

"Cast _your_ burden on the LORD,
And He shall sustain you; He shall
never permit the righteous to be moved."
(Psalms 55:22)

Hymns

Hymns are songs of worship and declaration to God we mistakenly think of as just "old time religion" songs early Christian sang _about_ God… but not _to_ God. That couldn't be farther from the truth!

Jesus sang hymns! On the night He was betrayed, in the final moments with His disciples in the upper room:

"And when they had sung a hymn,
they went out to the Mount of Olives."
(Matthew 26:30)

Some of the most prolific worship songs throughout Christianity were actually hymns written in the midst of the author's perilous storms. Here are several brief examples:

Amazing Grace. John Newton was a ruthless, slave-trader, blasphemer, immoral, torturer and vile man. In the midst of a great storm at sea, likely facing death, he got on his knees and pled to God for Mercy & Grace. Totally transformed by it, he wrote the song years later while pastoring in Olney, England.

How Great Thou Art. Carl Gustav Boberg was caught in a severe storm, frightened and hiding in a perch. He witnessed incredible thunder and lightning as the dark tempest passed over. Soon after, he saw the most beautiful rainbow set over the bay, with the sun shining and the birds chirping and the church bells softly tolling… Overwhelmed by God's greatness and Majesty (and deliverance) he penned this song.

'Tis So Sweet To Trust In Jesus. Louisa Stead wrote this incredibly popular hymn right after experiencing the most tragic death of her husband who drowned trying to save a young boy who was drowning off of Long Island, New York. Afterwards she ended up joining her daughter in missionary work in Africa for 25 years where her *song* is still sang in many different languages…

Through It All. Andrae Crouch had fallen in love with one of the young women who had joined his singing group called The Disciples. She was a featured soloist and often sang duets with Andrae. Without warning one Saturday morning she notified Andrae she was leaving the group and joining another singing group who travelled overseas. Heartbroken at the loss, Andrae penned the first two parts of the song. Feeling there was yet a closing part, he prayed earnestly for the Lord to give him that third and final part. Three weeks later the Lord provided the inspiration for that part. Just as he was finishing the very last part in the wee hours of the morning, (February 9, 1971), Andrae felt his room begin to shake, a violent earthquake struck the San Fernando Valley killing 64 people and causing over a billion dollars in damage.

Leaning On The Everlasting Arms. Minister and music teacher Anthony Showalter received letters from two previous students who had attended his music school just weeks before. Both had reported to him that their wives had died. As he thought about a word of comfort for both men, a Scripture came to mind:

"The eternal God is your refuge, and
underneath are the everlasting arms."
(Deuteronomy 33:27)

He wrote down the chorus to this beloved hymn, but reached out to a well know hymn writer, Elisha Hoffman for help completing the stanzas.

I could go on and on of hundreds of beloved hymns and songs which were all birthed out of tragedy, sorrow and suffering – *songs* written in the night – the dark night of trial and testing.

Spiritual Songs

A *"spiritual song"* is best understood as a "Divinely inspired utterance" from the flow of the Holy Spirit. It is often structured poetically, like an "ode" but most often contains the very essence of psalms or hymns (although it is generally understood to be "a fresh, spontaneous *Song of the Lord*)."

Paul alluded to its origin as having come from the Holy Spirit:

"Let the message of Christ dwell among
you richly as you teach and admonish
one another with all wisdom through
psalms, hymns, and **songs from the Spirit**,
singing to God with gratitude in your hearts."
(Colossians 3:16)

"Well, my brothers and sisters, let's summarize.
When you meet together, **some will sing**, others

may teach, another will tell some special revelation
God has given, one will speak in tongues, and
another will interpret what is said. But everything
that is done is to strengthen all of you."
(1 Corinthians 14:26)

It is clear from the Word that the *intention* of God for giving
us spiritual songs through the agency of the Holy Spirit is to
strengthen and **edify** us. I believe this Grace operates both in
a personal and a corporate flow as He (The Holy Spirit) wills,
just like all of the other gifts of the Holy Spirit.

"But one and the same Spirit works all these things,
distributing to each one **individually** as He wills."
(1 Corinthians 12:11)

In the very place where *your* present storm may be assailing
you, lift up high praise unto the Lord, and let the Spirit of God
come down in to the situation, in a special and powerful way
and He will "inhabit" that praise… (fusion).

As you do, as I have said before… faith will begin to arise.
Boldness will develop within *you* come before the Throne of
Grace. Boldness comes when you begin to encounter the
revelation of your association and union with Christ and
realize Jesus *is* going to move on *your* behalf! For you are *one*
with Him!!

"But he who is *joined* to the Lord is
 one spirit with Christ Jesus."
(1 Corinthians 6:17)

That is *fusion* my friend… And in that place of *confluence*, you will *experience* the Spirit of God begin to release the fresh *Song of the Lord* into your heart, whereupon in confidence you can sing right into <u>your</u> storm, declaring the intentionality of God's plan and purpose… Healing… Deliverance… Triumph… Freedom… Breakthrough… Provision… Wisdom… Comfort etc.

Praise will fill your lamp with oil to burn all through the *night seasons* of your life. It will also stir up faith… The enemy of your soul will do everything to try and get you to keep your eyes upon the waves (circumstances) so as to try and hinder and discourage you from *abiding* in a place of high praise.

Breakthrough is yours – right now, begin to move into praise… and don't stop – never stop!!!

ADMONISH ONE ANOTHER WITH ALL WISDOM,

SINGING PSALMS, HYMNS AND SPIRITUAL SONGS,

MAKING MELODY IN <u>YOUR</u> HEART…

EPHESIANS 5:19

THE SONGS OF WAR

"HE LEADS ME IN HIS TRIUMPH"

It is extremely important when a storm appears on your horizon to try and discern what the "source" of the storm is. In other words where did the storm originate?

Storms can come forth through a number of reasons like bad choices on our part that result in difficult consequences, from the hands of other people (intentionally or even unintentionally), through tragic accidents or unforeseen circumstances that arise in the cycles of everyday life, from personal loss, or hard times – the list could go on and on…

Yet the "source" could very well be the result of a direct demonic attack or assignment specifically intended towards *you*! It is important to know the difference… Why?

"…So that you may wage a good warfare."
(1 Timothy 1:18)

When you discern (through the help of the Holy Spirit) that the present storm you are encountering is truly the work of a demonic attack set against you – the principles and protocols found in this chapter will help you to overcome the plans of the enemy of your soul – and bring tremendous Glory to God!

For too long, we as Christians have curled up like a potato bug in the midst of adversity – living out our journey from a defensive posture… Hiding in the winepress like Gideon!

Satan and his cohorts have had a field day against man for far too long! Satan has employed his incredible craftiness through the work of his silver tongue to usurp God given authority that was originally assigned to man.

It started in the Garden of Eden. God delegated authority and rule over the entire earth to Adam.

"Then God said, "Let Us make man in
 Our image, according to Our likeness;
let them have dominion over the fish of
the sea, over the birds of the air, and over
the cattle, **over all the earth** and over every
creeping thing that creeps on the earth."
(Genesis 1:26)

We also understand that at the *fall* of Adam and Eve, they relinquished that authority and rule that had been entrusted to them. Satan usurped their authority that had been Adam's. Jesus confirmed this authority had been stolen by Satan...

"Now is the judgment of this world;
now the **ruler of this world** will be cast out."
(John 12:31)

Satan too confirmed it when he was tempting Jesus at the end of His 40 day fast...

"Then the devil, taking Him up on a high
mountain, showed Him all the kingdoms
of the world in a moment of time. And the
devil said to Him, "All this **authority** I will
give You, and their glory; **for *this* has been**

delivered to me, and I give it to whomever I
wish. Therefore, if You will worship before
me, all will be Yours."
(Luke 4:5-7)

And our enemy has continued to badger and make a mockery
of man ever since… Attacking him as an accuser (guilt,
shame, condemnation etc.) or attacking him as a tempter,
offering pleasures of wickedness – the fullness of what we see
in this fallen world.

Yet most of his accomplishments has come through lies,
deceit and smoking mirrors. He is like the Wizard of Oz
appearing in *our perspective* (eyesight and estimation) as the
great (terrible) and powerful Oz (up on the movie screen),
when in *reality* he is just a shriveled up fallen angel hiding
behind a curtain operating an incredible assortment of bells
and controls to fool and foil mankind! The Bible says we will
be astonished when we see him as he **really** is:

"Those who see you will gaze at you,
and consider you, saying: Is this the
man who made the earth tremble,
who shook kingdoms, who made the
world as a wilderness and destroyed its cities…"
(Isaiah 14:16-17)

We have been duped… When Satan sends category 5
hurricane storms to assail you – *you* have resolve! The Lord
has provided us everything *you* need – He declares it!!

"…As His divine power has *given* to us
all things that pertain to *life* and *godliness,*

through the knowledge of Him who called
us by glory and virtue…"
(2 Peter 1:3)

"Has given us…" meaning past tense (has _already_ happened). He has given us **everything** we need to overcome life's challenges and hardships in order to live a Godly lifestyle before the Lord - even though we know we are fighting a constant war for which there can be no truce…

The Lord has endued us with dunamis power from on high in the Holy Spirit, provided us with battle amour, given us mighty spiritual weapons that are not carnal (like the Word of God, the Blood of Jesus, and the Name of Jesus), the assistance of heavenly angels, and battle strategies (blueprints of Heaven).. He will also give us Wisdom – if we o_nly_ ask…

There is a warfare we can wage in worship! We can war in _song_ and in _dance_ unto the Lord! We can become overcomers through our storm with high praise! This is not only our calling – it is our heritage! Learn to _sing_ into your storm!

You were created to triumph victoriously! It's _your_ heritage!

"Praise the LORD!
Sing to the LORD a new song,
and His praise in the assembly of saints.

Let Israel rejoice in their Maker;
let the children of Zion be joyful in their King.
Let them praise His name with the _dance_;
let them _sing_ praises to Him with the timbrel and harp.

For the LORD takes pleasure in His people;
He will beautify the humble with salvation.

Let the saints be joyful in glory;
let them *sing* aloud on their beds.
Let the high praises of God be in their mouth,
and a two-edged sword in their hand,
to execute vengeance on the nations,
and punishments on the peoples;
to bind their kings with chains,
and their nobles with fetters of iron;
to execute on them the written judgment—
this honor have all His saints.
Praise the LORD!
(Psalms 149)

This instruction from the Word of God is not a defensive position against the attacks (storms) from our enemy. It is a mandate from God to move into high praise and war against our adversary! God has given us the call... and the weapons!

If that were not enough... look what the Lord does:

"Blessed be the LORD my Rock,
who **trains my hands for war,
and my fingers for battle**."
(Psalms 144:1)

Though the battle belongs to the Lord, we are His chosen instruments in the earth to do His bidding:

"**_You_** are My battle-ax and weapons of war:
For with **_you_** I will break the nation in pieces;
With **_you_** I will destroy kingdoms;
With **_you_** I will break in pieces the horse and its rider;
With **_you_** I will break in pieces the chariot and its rider;
With **_you_** also I will break in pieces man and woman;
With **_you_** I will break in pieces old and young;
With **_you_** I will break in pieces the young man and the
maiden;
With **_you_** also I will break in pieces the shepherd and his
flock;
With **_you_** I will break in pieces the farmer and his yoke of
oxen;
And with **_you_** I will break in pieces governors and rulers.
And I will repay Babylon…"
(Jeremiah 51:20-24)

The Lord is looking for a people who can stand in the day of
battle (storms) and remain faithful in Him (trusting and
loyal). The storms we encounter in our life can be Divine
opportunities to make us stronger and more resolute in God.

"For the eyes of the LORD run to and fro
throughout the whole earth, to show
Himself **strong** on behalf of _those_ whose
heart is loyal to Him."
(2 Chronicles 16:9)

There is a distinct process of preparation the Lord will take us
through in life (or allow) to season us into becoming a part of
the army of God. We must embrace His process and keep our
eyes on Him so that we don't become like the children of
Ephraim.

"The children of Ephraim, being armed and carrying bows, **turned back in the day of battle**. They did not keep the covenant of God; they refused to walk in His law, and forgot His works and His wonders that He had shown them. (Psalms 78:9-11)

"For yet a little while, and He who is coming will come and will not tarry. Now the **just shall live by faith**; but if *anyone* draws back, My soul has no pleasure in him." (Hebrews 10:37-38)

In order to stand or remain, we must learn how to properly be suited for the warfare we are encountering. Many who fail in this area are the very ones who did **NOT** dress for battle…

"Finally, my brethren, be **strong** in the Lord and in the power of His might. Put on the whole armor of God that you may be **able to stand** against the wiles of the devil. For we do not wrestle against flesh and blood, but against principalities, against powers, against the rulers of the darkness of this age, against spiritual hosts of wickedness in the heavenly places. Therefore take up the **whole armor of God** that you may be able to withstand in the evil day, and **having done all, to stand**." (Ephesians 6:10-13)

There is a great and amazing truth here we must understand. Overcoming faith for victorious Christian living doesn't depend on us – it depends on Jesus Christ! He is the one who got the victory on the cross. We are not fighting **FOR** a place of victory – we are fighting **FROM** a place of victory! In Christ we are **already** victorious!

"Now thanks be to God who **always** leads us
in triumph in Christ, and through _us_ diffuses
the fragrance of His knowledge in every place.
For _we_ are to God the fragrance of Christ among
those who are being saved and among those who
are perishing. To the one _we_ are the aroma of death
leading to death, and to the other the aroma of life
leading to life…
(2 Corinthians 2:14-16)

In this passage Paul is describing the procession of a Roman General just returning to the city of Rome after winning a great battle. The scene is that of a victory parade (which the Romans used to do) to commemorate the victory in war.

As soon as a victory was won by the Roman army, a messenger would be sent back to the city to proclaim the victory, and the people of that city would begin to prepare for the victory celebration (the victory parade).

The first people in the parade's procession were priests swinging chalices with burning incense, a special and fragrant incense only used during these types of processions. The next would be the musicians, playing songs of victory and celebration. Then next in line would be the soldiers of the battle, carrying with them the spoils of war they captured.

Then finally would come the conquering General who won the victory, riding in a beautiful golden chariot. Right behind him would be the defeated army's General or high ranking Commanders – who would be "**chained to his chariot**" and on public display.

Paul is using this analogy to describe the fact that _we_ too are being lead in a triumphal procession by our conquering General – Jesus Christ!! We are to be "**chained to His chariot!**" We are being lead forth in His (Christ's) triumphal procession it's not ours – it's His! (But only if we surrender to Him)…

That special fragrance of incense that Paul speaks of… To the one was the _aroma_ of death because when those chained to the chariot smelled that special incense they _knew_ they were being led to their deaths right after the victory parade. It was to them the _aroma_ of death…

But to the jubilant crowds - the fragrance of that special incense was the _aroma_ of life and victory! So to one it was the _aroma_ of death, to the other it was the _aroma_ of life…

We too are being led to our death (from self and dead works) into the victory that our Commander-in-Chief won at the cross! On one we hand there is the aroma of death – but in this case there is also a sweet fragrance unto the Lord…

We have been captured by His Love, being led forth as _prisoners_ of the Lord Jesus Christ (through voluntary surrender and obedience). As we have died to self, we are chained to His chariot and being led forth in His triumph (though many will also be led even further into martyrdom)

"Precious in the sight of the LORD
is the death of his saints."
(Psalms 116:15)

God wants to diffuse (release) the fragrance of Christ from us in every situation – to all people…

Remember the battle is not yours – it's the Lord's! He will deliver _you_! Stay chained to His chariot, with _your_ eyes upon Jesus, and a heart that places all of _your_ trust upon the Lord. You may be in the land of giants right now, but take heart like David did when he proclaimed:

"Then David said to the Philistine, "You come
to me with a sword, with a spear, and with a
javelin? **But I come to you in the name of the
LORD of hosts**, the God of the armies of Israel,
whom you have defied. This day the LORD will
deliver you into my hand, and I will strike you
and take your head from you. And this day I will
give the carcasses of the camp of the Philistines to
the birds of the air and the wild beasts of the earth,
that all the earth may know that there is a God in
Israel. Then all this assembly shall know that the
LORD does not save with sword and spear;
for the battle _is_ the LORD's, and He **will**
give you into our hands."
(1 Samuel 17:45-47)

Let the word of God dwell richly in you!! Let faith arise in your heart unto the Lord and His might provision! By faith you can be of a different spirit – like Caleb who declared:

"Then Caleb quieted the people before Moses,
and said, Let us go up at once and take
possession, for we are well **able to overcome** it."
(Numbers 13:30)

You too shall be an overcomer!! Lift up your *song* to the Lord!
Are you are chained to His chariot!

ARE YOU CHAINED
TO HIS CHARIOT?

THE SONG OF SONGS

THE MOUNTAIN OF MYRRH
THE HILL OF FRANKINCENSE

Solomon was a very prolific, prophetic and gifted song writer. The Bible says that he wrote over 1,000 songs, including *"The Songs of Solomon"*.

This incredible book is translated and called by several names including: Songs of Solomon, The Canticles etc., but the most popular translation is *The Song of Songs*, which better said is translated as *The Song of <u>all</u> Songs*.

Imagine for a moment why the Holy Spirit would inspire King Solomon to call it by that name... When you see a double emphasis in the Bible it clearly denotes the highest honor i.e. King of Kings... Holy of Holies... Song of <u>all</u> Songs...

By sheer title alone, this book should warrant our attention and study. There are truths contained within this work that can greatly help us to process and understand the trials, storms and suffering we incur throughout our Christian walk.

Although the book is a natural love song that magnifies the beauty of married love, it has far deeper spiritual significance that can help us to see the progression of holy passion for Christ through the workings of adversity in the life of His Bride to ultimately bring forth pure and holy love.

That process towards *perfected love* is the entire reason for our creation and our journey – it is the highest purpose in this life! Paul Billheimer in his most excellent book "Destined for the

Throne" shares one of the best descriptions for the purpose of creation that I have ever read:

"The primary purpose of the universe… is the production and preparation of an Eternal Companion for the Son", and that "since she is to share the throne of the universe with her Divine Lover and Lord… she must be trained… for that role".

THE GARDEN OF GETIISEMANE

During the course of our Christian walk, the Lord takes us through a journey (or process) to develop our hearts towards holy and pure passion for Him. In the early stages our hearts our immature and well rooted in *"self"* (our own interests) while our mental rationale (decision making) is operated by and through our own inspiration and self *"will"*.

The adversities (storms) that the Lord *allows* to touch our lives (Some storms He generates, some He allows, but He can work in and through them **all**) have distinct *purpose* to cultivate the soil of our heart, breaking up hard ground (hardness of heart), uprooting weeds etc…

It is all intended to bring our immature hearts into union with His, in order to deepen our love and dependence upon Jesus our Bridegroom King.

In this life all true Christians we will surely experience at sundry times what we shall call a *season* in the Garden of Gethsemane… The word Gethsemane itself means "oil press or winepress". It is a *place* where olives are put into the press and then *crushed* to extract forth the oil… It was used in the first stage of the making of anointing oil… *crushing* to bring forth the precious oil - that could not come by any other way.

Although Gethsemane was spoken in Greek, its word origin "gath" is actually of Aramaic language dating back through the Old Testament denoting "winepress". But it too carries the same implications… in order to make *new wine*, it starts by the *crushing* of grapes. Placing the grapes in the winepress and pressing to draw forth the blood of the grapes…

There is a parallel here that can help us to understand some of the processes of God in our lives. When we experience a Gethsemane season in our lives - where we are placed in the oil press of God – it is there in that place that the Lord *presses* our lives to bring forth a sweet and pure oil that can then be made into precious anointing oil.

Another picture of Gethsemane is the place where God places us in the winepress to *press* and extract the precious juice, suitable for the making of new wine. What comes forth is pleasant to God. It's just like in order to make the sweetest and fragrant perfume – it <u>first</u> requires the *crushing* of the rose (flower) petals to eventually bring forth the sweet fragrance!

When we better understand the processes God takes us through – <u>and His ultimate *purpose* in them</u>, we can learn to cooperate with Him much better and garner the full *benefits* of our storms and what they are capable of producing in our lives i.e. deeper intimacy with Christ (pure and Holy passion for Him), a stronger, more active faith, and a *powerful* testimony glorifies God and encourages and strengthens others when they are encountering *their* Gethsemane…

This process is capable of producing the beautiful fruit of the Spirit in our lives, and all of the chief spices that are major ingredients in the holy anointing oil. So much so that our King may desire our beauty and come and eat of the sweet, ripened fruit in His garden…"

"So the King will greatly desire your beauty;
Because He *is* your Lord, worship Him.
And the daughter of Tyre *will come* with a gift;
The rich among the people will seek your favor.
The royal daughter *is* all glorious within *the palace;*
Her clothing *is* woven with gold.
She shall be brought to the King in robes of many colors;
The virgins, her companions who follow her, shall be
brought to You. With gladness and rejoicing they shall be
brought; they shall enter the King's palace."
(Psalms 45:11-15)

But our love for Him is still immature and not fully
developed. For we still have "walls" built up in our life and
our hearts are still divided (compartmentalized) with our
own interests, wounds, and even hidden faults.

In this the Lord comes to us – in the night season (storms). He
comes with the intent to bring us through our storms – and
into deepened Love if we will _go_ with Him through faith and
obedience…

"The voice of my Beloved!
Behold, He comes
Leaping upon the mountains,
Skipping upon the hills.
My beloved is like a gazelle or a young stag.
Behold, He stands behind **our wall**;
He is looking through _our_ windows,
Gazing through _our_ lattice.
My Beloved spoke, and said to me:
Rise up, My love, My fair one,
And come away.
For lo, the winter is past,

The rain is over and gone.
The flowers appear on the earth;
The time of *singing* has come,
And the voice of the turtledove
Is heard in our land.
The fig tree puts forth her green figs,
And the vines with the tender grapes
Give a pleasant smell.
Rise up, My love, My fair one,
And come away!
O My dove, in the clefts of the rock,
In the secret places of the cliff,
Let Me see your *face*,
Let Me hear your *voice*;
For your *voice* is sweet,
And your *face* is lovely."
(Song of Songs 2:8-14)

What an incredible word picture and story! The Shulamite woman is already in love with Him as seen in the first chapter one *"the Song of all Songs."*

But in the night season, He comes beckoning her to rise up (from the night) and come away with Him… Her deliverance has come! He declares to her the storm has passed, and the winter (bitter elements) is over. He tells her that it is **now** springtime and the flowers are appearing on the earth and it *is the time for singing*!

He is telling her in the midst of her dark night that He has *made a way* for her and invites her to *come* with Him. Even though she is **still** in the midst of the night. He is already telling her that season is over and it is now springtime and He tells her it is time to begin *singing* (even in the midst of her night) – even <u>before</u> it has physically manifested in her life! She is *invited* to go with Him by faith…

Though the Lord's love for her is very strong, and He can easily leap over mountains and skip upon the hills – He will not leap over her <u>**walls**</u>. She tells Him she loves Him – but she did <u>**not**</u> go with Him!

"My beloved *is* mine, and I *am* his.
He feeds *His flock* among the lilies.
Until the day breaks
And the shadows flee away,
Turn, my Beloved,
And be like a gazelle
Or a young stag
Upon the mountains of Bether."
(Song of Songs 2:16, 17)

In her mindset day hasn't broken yet and the shadows are still there. She is still in her night…

This is often what we do in the midst of our storms. Being Christians, we go through the motions of spiritual protocols for handling trials, temptations and tragedies (as we have been taught) but somehow our faith doesn't seem to get full traction in the Spirit. We must go by faith when He calls!! Remember the 10 lepers who were healed??

"They were healed - <u>***as they went forth***</u>…"
(Luke 17:14)

The Shulamite woman remained "in the night" and by the time she decided to try and "*go*" with Him – the Divine opportunity for heartfelt faith had opened and closed… and He was gone. The opportunity was gone…

"By night on my bed I sought the one I love;
I sought Him, but I did not find Him. I will
rise now, I said, And go about the city; in
the streets and in the squares I will seek the
One I love, I sought Him, but I **did not** find Him."
(Song of Songs 3:1, 2)

Remember what the Beloved said? "Come with Me… Let Me hear _your_ voice… _Your_ voice is so sweet…It's time to _Sing_!" These storms are golden opportunity for the maturing of holy love for Him.
Don't waste your sorrows (They are Divine opportunities)… Could the Shulamite woman have come into that understanding? I think she did..In the next chapter we read:

"Do not stir up nor awaken
love _until_ it pleases."
(Song of Songs 3:5)

THE MOUNTAIN OF MYRRH

Love is fully _ready_ (mature) to please when it reaches the point of sacrificial devotion for another. The Scriptures tell us:

"_Greater_ love has no one than this…
than to _lay down_ one's life for his friends."
(John 15:13)

The Bible defines the _proof_ of God's love for us:

"But God demonstrated His own love toward
us, in that while we were _still_ sinners, Christ
died for us."
(Romans 5:8)

The _laying down_ of one's life for _another_ (Christ) is not meant to just be understood as physical death only. It is equally proportionate in coming to the place of the death of our self-will in exchange for the will of God.

That is how the term or phrase becoming _laid down lovers_ of Christ was coined. We come to the place of death, surrender and abandonment unto obedience and devotion unto God. Where did Jesus face the ultimate display of a confrontation between His will and the will of His Father? In the Garden of Gethsemane!

"Saying, Father, if thou be willing, remove
this cup from Me: nevertheless **_not_** my will,
but Thine, be done."
(Luke 22:42)

The Garden of Gethsemane is the place where the Lord brings us to begin to be _pressed_. It is the place of great trial and tribulations (storms). God's _purpose_ is to bring us through the Garden of Gethsemane and up into the Mountain of Myrrh.

Myrrh is a beautiful and fragrant ointment – but it is also the chief death spice or burial spice. Jesus' body was prepared with Myrrh at His death in preparation for His burial.

Myrrh translated is the Hebrew word "_mor_". It is understood by most Bible Scholars that the Mountain of Myrrh most likely refers to Mt. Moriah. Where was the Garden of Gethsemane? On the Mount of Olives – which is Mt. Moriah (better said *upper* Mt. Moriah). The place of death, the place of sacrifice…

It was the very *same* place where God instructed Abraham to bring his son to and build and altar there to *sacrifice* him something like 1800 years before Christ.
Just as Abraham was about to sacrifice Isaac, a ram suddenly appeared in the thickets, fulfilling what Abraham already knew:

"…God will provide for Himself the
lamb for a burnt offering."
(Genesis 22:8)

It is well argued that the *same* place (area) where the ram appeared (a type and shadow of the crucifixion of Christ) on Mt. Moriah was also the exact place where the crucifixion of Christ took place nearly two millennia later on the Mt. of Olives!

We too are called *spiritually* up to Mt. Moriah – the Mountain of Myrrh. We too must follow Christ *through* the Garden of Gethsemane (*pressing, crushing*) and up to the Mountain of Myrrh (the place of death) and embrace <u>our</u> cross (the cross of death to self). Jesus requires this of His true followers!

"Then Jesus said to His disciples, "If <u>*anyone*</u>
 desires to come after Me, let him <u>*deny*</u> himself,
and <u>take up his cross</u>, and <u>*follow*</u> Me."
(Matthew 16:24)

The storms in your life help bring you to Gethsemane. Surrendering them fully unto God and embracing His will in the midst of _your_ dark night (through faith and obedience) – **no matter what the outcome of the trial or tribulation may be**, represents the further transition of moving _beyond_ the Garden of Gethsemane and up into the Mountain of Myrrh as His _laid down lover_ – one who is coming to the place of fully surrendering to the will of God.

This was the course the Shulamite woman ended up taking eventually… Awaiting her breakthrough (better said - the outcome from her dark night).

"_Until_ the day breaks, and the shadows flee
away, I will _go_ my way to the mountain of
myrrh, and to the hill of frankincense."
(Song of Songs 4:6)

The expression of the word "Myrrh" is used in the _Song of Songs_ more than any other book in the Bible – as a matter of fact… five times more. Look at the power of sacrificial love, a love proven by death!

"Set me as a Seal upon Your heart, as a
Seal upon Your arm; For (this) love _is_ as
strong as death, jealousy as cruel as the
grave; its flames are flames of _fire_, a most
vehement flame."
(Song of Songs 8:6)

THE HILL OF FRANKINCENSE

This speaks of coming up into a deeper place of prayer and intercession up in the hill of the Lord. Again, traditionally this place… The Mountain of Myrrh and the Hill of Frankincense is understood to be Mt. Moriah. Jesus knew this place very well, for He often went there to *pray*, seeking the will of His Father…

"And in the daytime He was teaching in
the temple, but at night He went out and
stayed on the mountain called Olives."
(Luke 21:37)

"…He went to the Mount of Olives, as He
was accustomed to, and His disciples also
followed Him."
(Luke 22:39)

As we come up to the Mountain of Myrrh, in the posture of death to our self-will (and all its wants, desires, ambitions, and motives etc.), we are much better positioned to deeply encounter God in a place of *prayer* – burning as a sweet and fragrant incense unto the Lord.

"Let my prayer be set before You as
incense, the lifting up of my hands as
the evening *sacrifice*."
(Psalms 141:2)

The Hill of Frankincense is the place of sweet, fragrant prayer and fellowship with the Lord, where, through surrender unto Him, we are able to pray in true fellowship with Christ, void of our own *motives* and *mixtures*. That is why The Mountain of Myrrh and The Hill of Frankincense go hand in hand.

In the midst of our storms, we tend to cry out to God from a place of *fear* and *anxiety*, wanting Him to bend to our wants and needs (expectations) instead of us rather bending (bowing) to His…

It isn't that we don't ask – Scripture is clear about asking of God through prayer, but when self (or selfishness) is involved, we are in danger of praying incorrectly in our storms that could literally *nullify* the intended *purposes* that God intends to extract from these trials and tribulations.

Give unto to the Lord the sweet and pleasant aroma of prayer as frankincense, offered as a *laid down* lover of Jesus, fully yielding unto His will – being resolute in <u>*your*</u> heart, and full prepared to embrace His chosen outcome for the very storm that is now touching <u>*your*</u> life!

I AM *my beloved's,* AND MY *beloved is mine.*

Song of Solomon 6:3

THE SONG OF DAVID II

"THE THUNDERING'S OF HEAVEN"

When we choose **praise** in the midst of our battle (storms) it deeply affects the living God and it can *move* Heaven on <u>your</u> behalf! God is no respecter of persons or one who shows partiality of any kind. He loves <u>you</u> every bit as much as He loved King David…

David was a man acutely aware of trials, tribulations, tragedies and – injustice… He made colossal mistakes and poor choices throughout his life – (just as we have) – but he also *moved* Heaven - so please be encouraged by this chapter!

David offered unto the Lord a reflective (account) *songs* of praise, adoration, remembrance and declaration of the faithfulness, power and majesty of God. It is called *The Song of David*. This is a classic *song* to begin to *sing* unto to the Lord, whether the black tempest in your life is just beginning to cross your path or even if you are already in the midst of the *eye of the storm*…

David opens his *song* with a declaration about the **safety** and **deliverance** he has found in God – this as a great place for <u>you</u> to open up <u>your</u> *song* to the Lord!

"The LORD *is* my <u>rock</u> and my <u>fortress</u> and my <u>deliverer</u>;
The God of my <u>strength</u>, in whom I will trust;
My <u>shield</u> and the <u>horn</u> of my salvation,
My <u>stronghold</u> and my <u>refuge</u>;
My <u>Savior</u>, You save me from violence.
I will call upon the LORD, who is *worthy* to be praised;

So shall I be saved from my enemies.
(2 Samuel 22:1-4)

The next part of David's song is his **testimony**. David testifies in the **power** of testimony as to the faithfulness of God, the conditions he found himself in and God's response… _You_ too have a testimony in your life where God may have provided for you miraculously, healed you, delivered you, intervened, answered your prayers, and sent help from His Sanctuary etc.

Like David, begin to _sing_ unto the Lord declaratively and historically what He has _already_ done for you – in the power of testimony! It releases fresh faith from _your_ heart!

"When the waves of death surrounded me,
The floods of ungodliness made me afraid.
The sorrows of Sheol surrounded me;
The snares of death confronted me.
In my distress I _called_ upon the LORD,
And _cried_ out to my God;
He _heard_ my voice from His temple,
And my cry _entered_ His ears.
(2 Samuel 22:5-7)

When _you_ choose to **praise** God in _your_ storm and fully trust Him (in faith and purity) <u>for the outcome of His choosing</u> – _you_ too can move Heaven in _your_ favor! _You_ too can _rouse_ God in jealousy from His Holy habitation!

"Then the earth shook and trembled;
The foundations of Heaven quaked and were shaken,
Because He was angry.
Smoke went up from His nostrils,
And devouring fire from His mouth;
Coals were kindled by it.

He bowed the heavens also, and came down
With darkness under His feet.
He rode upon a cherub, and flew;
And He was seen upon the wings of the wind.
He made darkness canopies around Him,
Dark waters and thick clouds of the skies.
From the brightness before Him
Coals of fire were kindled.
The LORD *thundered* from heaven,
And the Most High uttered His voice.
He sent out arrows and scattered them;
Lightning bolts, and He vanquished them.
Then the channels of the sea were seen,
The foundations of the world were uncovered,
At the rebuke of the LORD,
At the blast of the breath of His nostrils.
(2 Samuel 22:8-16)

Does that mean in every storm I encounter I just have to simply **praise** God and He will move like this from Heaven? I would say you don't know what the Lord will do on *your* behalf! Don't limit the Holy One of Israel! Let God be God!

Our part in any storm is to take our eyes *off* the *waves* and focus our attention upon Jesus. If you can learn to truly take your eyes off the *waves* (circumstances) then *you* can become un-wave-ering (unwavering) and *resolute* upon God!

In David's song, he continues on with his testimony of God's awesome power, kindness and delivering hand. Our God is a God of deliverance! He is faithful to all generations!

"He sent from above, He took me,
He drew me out of many waters.
He delivered me from my strong enemy,
From those who hated me;
For they were too strong for me.
They confronted me in the day of my calamity,
But the LORD was my support.
He also brought me out into a broad place;
He delivered me because He delighted in me.
(2 Samuel 22:17-20)

Imagine that!! God was delighted in David! A man who was a poor father role at best, an adulterer (Bathsheba), a murderer (Uriah), and a man whose pride and presumption took an unauthorized census that directly caused the deaths of 70,000 people! Yet through God's kindness, forgiveness and purifying power, look on what basis David's attributes his deliverance from:

"The LORD rewarded me according to my righteousness;
According to the cleanness of my hands
He has recompensed me.
For I have kept the ways of the LORD,
And have not wickedly departed from my God.
For all His judgments were before me;
And as for His statutes, I did not depart from them.
I was also blameless before Him,
And I kept myself from my iniquity.
Therefore the LORD has recompensed me
According to my righteousness,
According to my cleanness in His eyes.
With the merciful You will show Yourself merciful;
With a blameless man You will show Yourself blameless;

With the pure You will show Yourself pure;
And with the devious You will show Yourself shrewd.
You will save the humble people;
But Your eyes are on the haughty,
That You may bring them down.
(2 Samuel 22:21-28)

Are we talking about the same man? That is how powerful God can cleanse each one of us and develop a **testimony** in us, just like David through Gods' saving grace...

God so thoroughly cleansed David's life that He was even able to bring forth the very lineage of Christ through his adulterous marriage to Bathsheba (Solomon's Mother)!

What separated King David from King Saul? For David acted just as unrighteously as King Saul – but David *knew* of the mercifulness of God, and David had a tender heart that was *quick* to repent unto the Lord. David leaned of the power and importance of God's Word – and learned to hide it in his heart… so that he may not sin (that is continuously…)

"For You are my lamp, O LORD;
The LORD shall enlighten my darkness.
For by You I can run against a troop;
By my God I can leap over a wall.
As for God, His way is perfect;
The word of the LORD *is* proven;
He is a shield to all who **_trust_** in Him.
For who is God, except the LORD?
And who is a rock, except our God?
God is my strength and power,
And He makes my way perfect.

He makes my feet like the feet of deer,
And sets me on my high places.
He teaches my hands to make war,
So that my arms __can__ bend a bow of bronze.
You have also given me the shield of Your salvation;
Your gentleness has made me great.
You enlarged my path under me;
So my feet did not slip.
(2 Samuel 22:29-37)

With our hearts cleansed, and our faith sure, great confidence in God's ability to navigate us through each storm is within reach!

God will not only *make* a way for us – God will *lead* us in the way! His Word is a **lamp** unto our feet and a **light** unto our path. Our safest and surest path in the midst of a storm is to *follow* Him…

If we *truly* trust in Him, then He will guide us by the Word and by the Spirit. He will illuminate your path! Ask the Lord to *speak* to you! Hear the voice of the Lord!

"Man shall not *live* by bread alone, but
by every Word (Rhema) that proceeds
from the mouth of God."
(Matthew 4:4)

"I have pursued my enemies and destroyed them;
Neither did I turn back again till they were destroyed.
And I have destroyed them and wounded them,
So that they could not rise;
They have fallen under my feet.

For You have armed me with strength for the battle;
You have subdued under me those who rose against me.
You have also given me the necks of my enemies,
So that I destroyed those who hated me.
They looked, but there was none to save;
Even to the LORD, but He did not answer them.
Then I beat them as fine as the dust of the earth;
I trod them like dirt in the streets,
And I spread them out."
(2 Samuel 22:38-43)

The beginning of a storm can also be the beginning of a mighty deliverance, a great victory and a powerful testimony! But you must be properly dressed for battle and properly armed! Let's look at the check list of *your* Holy attire:

1) Clothed in humility.
2) Garment of praise.
3) Robe of righteousness
4) Mantle of power.
5) Necklace (pearls) of wisdom.
6) A Signet ring.

We know that in many storms we engage as a Christian, that we are not wrestling against flesh and blood, but against principalities, powers, might's, dominions etc. against the very hordes of hell. Whether the attack is a direct demonic assault against you or working through other people and situations – you must be properly armed for battle. According to the Word of God let's check our armor:

1. Belt of Truth.
2. Shod feet – Gospel ready.

3. Shield of faith.
4. Helmet of Salvation.
5. Sword of the Spirit.
6. Continuous Prayer & Supplication

But we must also have our mental and emotional focus set upon the Lord, fully prepared… Our final checklist:

1. Girded up loins (of our mind).
2. Mind of Christ.
3. Unoffendable hearts.
4. Active faith.
5. Agape' Love.
6. Joy.
7. Peace.
8. Longsuffering.
9. Kindness.
10. Goodness.
11. Faithfulness.
12. Gentleness.
13. Self-control.

There is far more involved in being adequately prepared for fierce storms than one imagines. Some storms pass over quickly, but others can be lengthy and endearing… We don't know how long each storm will last – but we do know the One who does know…

The more we trust Him, yield to Him, seek Him, and utilize the tools, weapons and endowments He has given us – the more successful we will be persevering through the storms, giving Glory to God, growing personally, and experiencing great victories!

It is my prayer for you that like David, when you come to the other side of your storm – _your_ song in the storm will end up just like this:

"The LORD lives!
Blessed _be_ my Rock!
Let God be exalted,
The Rock of my salvation!
It is God who avenges me,
and subdues the peoples under me;
He delivers me from my enemies.
You also lift me up above those
who rise against me; You have delivered
me from the violent man. Therefore I
will give thanks to You, O LORD, among
 the Gentiles, and _sing_ praises to Your
name. He is the tower of salvation to
His king, and shows mercy to His anointed,
To David and his descendants forevermore."
(2 Samuel 22: 47-51)

COME SING A NEW SONG OF DAVID!!

THE SONG OF MOSES

"FAITHFULNESS VS. JUDGMENT"

It is quite amazing to see the opening of Revelation 15 with a picture of Angels of Judgment readying the last 7 plagues to be poured out that contain the complete (final) wrath of God.

"Then I saw another sign in heaven,
great and marvelous: seven angels
having the seven last plagues, for in
them the wrath of God is complete."
(Revelation 15:1)

A frightful picture… But then the scene opens up further to John and he sees an incredible sight!

"And I saw something like a sea of glass
mingled with fire, and those who have
the victory over the beast, over his image
and over his mark and over the number
of his name, standing on the sea of glass,
having harps of God. They *sing The Song
of Moses*, the servant of God, and *The Song
of the Lamb*, saying:

Great and marvelous are Your works,
Lord God Almighty! Just and true are
Your ways, O King of the saints!
Who shall not fear You, O Lord, and
glorify Your name?" For You alone are holy.
For all nations shall come and worship
before You, for Your judgments have

been manifested."
(Revelation 15:2-4

What a dichotomy of events at the same time! Final judgment is about to be poured out upon the earth and simultaneously, a company of saints are *singing victoriously* unto the Lord God Almighty declaring how great and awesome His *works* and His *ways* are... Fearfully and reverently engulfed in His Majesty and His Holiness – they are in perfect agreement and harmony with Him concerning the judgments being released!

The children of Israel are approaching the Promised Land after wanderings in the wilderness for nearly 40 years. As they approach Mt. Nebo the Lord tells Moses he is about to die. He has him officially set Joshua in as the new leader as He instructs Moses to write *The Song of Moses* – one of the last things Moses did in his life…

The Song of Moses was a poetic, (and very prophetic) *song* forecasting the direction Israel would <u>choose</u> to go in those days i.e. after other gods, playing the harlot and breaking covenant with the true and living God.

And the LORD said to Moses:

"Behold, you will rest with your fathers;
and this people will rise and play the harlot
with the gods of the foreigners of the land,
where they go to be among them, and they
will forsake Me and break My covenant
which I have made with them. Then My anger
shall be aroused against them in that day, and
I will forsake them, and I will hide My face from
them, and they shall be devoured. And many evils
and troubles shall befall them, so that they will say

in that day, Have not these evils come upon us because our God is not among us? And I will surely hide My face in that day because of all the evil which they have done, in that they have turned to other gods.

Now therefore, **write down this song for yourselves**, and teach it to the children of Israel; put it in their mouths, **that this song may be a witness for Me** against the children of Israel. (Deuteronomy 31: 16-19)

Not only did this song has short range prophetic fulfillment, but it also included long range prophetic insight and relevancy even into our day!

"For I know that after my death you will become utterly corrupt, and turn aside from the way which I have commanded you. And evil will befall you **in the latter days**, because you will do evil in the sight of the LORD, to provoke Him to anger through the work of your hands." (Deuteronomy 31:29)

The Song of Moses itself is the **testimony** of God's faithfulness and Love to Israel throughout history. It tells of how the Lord continually pursued them, protected them, and provided for them.

"He found him in a desert land
And in the wasteland, a howling wilderness;
He encircled him, He instructed him,
He kept him as the apple of His eye.
As an eagle stirs up its nest,
Hovers over its young,

Spreading out its wings, taking them up,
Carrying them on its wings,
So the Lord alone led him,
And there was no foreign god with him.
He made him ride in the heights of the earth,
That he might eat the produce of the fields;
He made him draw honey from the rock,
And oil from the flinty rock;
Curds from the cattle, and milk of the flock,
With fat of lambs;
And rams of the breed of Bashan, and goats,
With the choicest wheat;
And you drank wine, the blood of the grapes.
(Deuteronomy 32:10-14)

But they rejected the Lord and His covenantal Love, going after other gods, provoking God to both jealousy and anger. Their _choices_ brought upon themselves severe judgment.

"For they are a nation void of counsel,
nor is there any understanding in them.
Oh, that they were wise, that they
understood this, that they would
consider their latter end!"
(Deuteronomy 32:28-29)

"Is this not laid up in store with Me, sealed
up among My treasures? Vengeance is Mine,
and recompense; their foot shall slip in _due_
time; for the day of their calamity _is_ at hand,
And the things to come hasten upon them."
(Deuteronomy 32: 34-35)

On the one hand, there is great blessing, favor, protection, provision and power for those who Love their God and keep His Covenant. There is also great calamity, destruction and judgment for those seek other gods, idols… demons.

"Now see that I, even I, am He, and there
is no God besides Me; I kill and I make alive;
I wound and I heal; Nor is there any who can
deliver from My hand. For I raise My hand to
heaven, and say, As I live forever, if I whet My
glittering sword, and My hand takes hold on
judgment, I will render vengeance to My enemies,
and repay those who hate Me. I will make My
arrows drunk with blood, and My sword shall
devour flesh, with the blood of the slain and the
captives, from the heads of the leaders of the enemy."
(Deuteronomy 32:39-42)

The very foundation of the Throne of God (upon which He sits is made of *righteousness* and *justice* (judgement).

"Righteousness and justice are the
foundation of Your throne; Mercy
and Truth go before Your face."
(Psalms 89:14)

Our God is Holy & Just, and every judgment that He makes is pure and righteous all together. Oh if the peoples could only see the Love and compassion of the Lord, His tenderness, patience and long-suffering…

"For the LORD will judge His people, and
have compassion on His servants, when
He sees that their power is gone, and there
is no one remaining, bond or free."
(Deuteronomy 32:36)

"With the merciful You will show Yourself
merciful; With a blameless man You will
show Yourself blameless; With the pure
You will show Yourself pure; And with the
devious You will show Yourself shrewd.
For You will save the humble people, But
will bring down haughty looks."
(Psalms 18:25-27)

How great is our God!

"The LORD executes righteousness
And justice for all who are oppressed.
He made known His ways to Moses,
His acts to the children of Israel.
The LORD *is* merciful and gracious,
Slow to anger, and abounding in mercy.
He will not always strive with us,
Nor will He keep His anger forever.
He has not dealt with us according to our sins,
Nor punished us according to our iniquities.
For as the heavens are high above the earth,
So great is His mercy toward those who fear Him;
As far as the east is from the west,
So far has He removed our transgressions from us.
As a father pities his children,
So the LORD pities those who fear Him.
For He knows our frame;
He remembers that we are dust."
(Psalms 103:6-13)

So *The Song of Moses* closes with a powerful declaration of justice and a Messianic *promise* of deliverance through Christ.

"Rejoice, O Gentiles, with His people; for
He _will_ avenge the blood of His servants,
and render vengeance to His adversaries;
He will provide atonement for His land
and His people."
(Deuteronomy 32:43)

So how is _The Song of Moses_ relevant today to you? For those who choose to live by faith (the just) in obedience to the Lord, His _Word_ and His _Ways_ – we stand in His victory – not in His judgement!

In the midst of your fiery trials, tribulations and all-out assault from the enemy of your souls – you have the privilege and the honor to be able to sing _The Song of Moses_ and _The Song of the Lamb_!

Remember that company of Saints in Revelation 15 who had harps given to them by God so they could _sing…._ _The Song of Moses_ and _The Song of the Lamb_? You don't have to wait until you have reached Heaven to join in those _songs_!

We stand at the brink of Great Tribulation now! No matter what type of storms are assailing you – lift up your head for your Redemption draws nigh! Lift up your _song_ – for the Lord will either deliver you or avenge you – it's all unto His Glory!

You are part of the His victorious company! You are an overcomer! You overcame by the Blood of the Lamb and by the Word (validity) of your Testimony.

Look at the exceeding promises in store for those who overcome. Does this look like something you might be interested in partaking of?

1) To eat from the **Tree of Life** in the midst of the Paradise of God.

2) To receive the **Crown of Life**.
3) To not be hurt by the **Second Death**.
4) To eat of God's **Hidden Manna**.
5) To be given a **White Stone** with a new name written on it nobody knows except the one who receives it.
6) To receive **Power over the Nations**.
7) To be given the **Morning Star**.
8) To be clothed in **White Garments**.
9) To have your name preserved in the **Book of Life**.
10) To have Jesus **Confess _your_ name** before His Father and all the Angels.
11) To be **kept from the hour of trial**, coming upon the whole earth.
12) To become a **Pillar in the Temple** of God and to never go out of that very place.
13) To have the **name of God written** on your forehead and the **name of the city of God**.
14) To have the **new name of Jesus** written upon you.
15) To be granted to **sit with Jesus on His Throne**.

This is a pretty incredible list of promises available to those who _overcome_ the storms of trial, temptation, and tragedy in their lives. You can be part of this company too!

The right to sing _The Song of Moses_ and _The Song of the Lamb_ among that victorious company stems from uncompromising faith, obedience, and worship of God.

That is why _The Song of Moses_ is so relevant today. Like in the days of Moses and the children of Israel, our faith will be tested and many will falter. Will you?

The _choice_ is absolutely _yours_! Will _you_ be _singing_ this _song_ in the end? Then learn how to _sing_ into your storms!

AND THEY SING
THE SONG OF MOSES &
THE SONG OF THE LAMB

REVELATION 15:3

THE SHIGGAION SONG

"STIRRED ZEAL – MIGHTY JUSTICE"

There is a type of Psalm (*song*) in the Bible that is perhaps of the most fervent and tenacious variety of any other kind of plea unto the Lord. It is only used twice in the Bible - in Psalms 7 and Habakkuk 3.

We are perhaps familiar with some of the different types of Psalms like a *"maskil"* (a skillful Psalm of wisdom or instruction) or perhaps a *"mikhtam"* (precious and impacting just like engraved gold).

But there is another type or fashion of a Psalm called *"shiggaion"* (pronounced sha-guy-yawn), meaning a "wild, mournful ode" or to "reel back and forth or stagger violently with deep emotional duress or passion."

It represents the deepest heartfelt emotional cry (*song*) unto the Lord, pleading for justice or breakthrough. In the case of Psalm 7 it is worshipful anguish from David unto the Lord on behalf of some great injustice done to him at the hands of Cush the Benjamite (as well as others).

A *"shiggaion"* could well be called *"The Song of the Slandered Saint"* as Charles Spurgeon calls it. Every Christian will have to encounter the pain and suffering of slander and personal attack (accusation) that can produce deep emotional trauma during their spiritual journey – it is inevitable...

David opens up Psalms 7 to lift his *"shiggaion"* (worshipful plea) unto the Lord against his accuser who has charged David with treason and treachery before King Saul (who himself was already in jealous outrage against David and wanted to take his life).

"O Lord my God, in You I put my trust;
Save me from all those who persecute me;
And deliver me, Lest they tear me like a lion,
Rending me in pieces, while there is none
to deliver.
(Psalms 7:1-2)

We too have an adversary who goes about as a roaring lion, seeking whom he might devour. Deep and personal attacks often come from other Christians which is why we refer to it as *friendly fire*. The worst response we can make is to harbor the impact of such vicious and devastating assaults unto ourselves and let an offense *build* in our heart. If we do, that *wound* can become *infected* and *grow* from resentment and hurt - into bitterness.

Unforgiveness is poison to our soul. It blocks God from moving in ways that could bring healing and deliverance to us in the situation (storm).

"For if you forgive men their trespasses,
your heavenly Father will also forgive *you*.
But if *you* do **not** forgive men their trespasses,
neither will your Father forgive your trespasses."
(Matthew 6:14-15)

There is a very powerful lesson to be learned here concerning offenses. Developing this very area of our Christian lives is paramount to spiritual growth, and will determine to what level we will actually bear fruit in lives. Just look at Scriptures about this:

"Woe to the world because of *offenses*!
For *offenses* must come, but woe to that
man through whom the offense comes!"
(Matthew 6:7)

The word for *offenses* is the Greek word *"skandalon"*. It is the exact same word from which we derive "scandal". It literally means *"the bait stick"* or the *"trap stick"*. It is the device in a mousetrap that triggers the trap to spring shut (upon your head)!

"Skandalon" itself isn't the cheese… The cheese is the offense or wound… When we bite (let the offense enrage us) – and let those arrows penetrat our heart to release their venom, we literally *"spring"* the *"skandalon"* upon ourselves and become trapped! Forgiveness *releases* us from the trap!

Unforgiveness is one of the major causes for division in the church and in our personal relationships. The importance of recognizing this debilitating factor and establishing unoffendable hearts towards God (and each other) is critical to fulfilling our destiny and call upon the earth. Many of the storms throughout your life will come as a result of *offense*. We must learn to *master* it (that is…give it to the Master…)

"This being so, I myself always strive to have a
conscience without *offense* toward God and men."
(Acts 24:16)

This is what David was doing… He was deeply hurt and overwhelmed by the attack from this guy named Cush. He turned his pain and agony, into lamentable, poetic, and worshipful plea unto the Lord through a *"shiggaion"* type *song*. We too can do the same – if we try… It is a matter of the heart… It's a _choice_… We either _choose_ to forgive… or to **not** forgive…

It is important to understand that choosing to forgive does **not** mean completing overlooking the serious of the attack or the forfeiting of any type of justice upon the one who has delivered the blow (wound) to you. That is the deeper part of the "shiggaion" – it is bringing the merits of the attack before the Lord and asking **Him** to judge righteously between both of you (or all parties concerned).

Our job is to not let anger consume us. Again, anger is a _choice_. It is said _anger_ is just one letter away from _danger_ – and rightly so… That is why the Word of God says:

"Be angry, but do not sin, **do not** let the sun go down on your wrath, nor _give place_ to the devil." (Ephesians 4:26-27)

"Let all bitterness, wrath, anger, clamor, and evil speaking be put away from you, with all malice. And be _kind_ to one another, _tenderhearted_, _forgiving_ one another, even as God in Christ also forgave _you_." (Ephesians 4:31-32)

In David's "_shiggaion_", he is approaching God in the purest posture of heart possible. He is pleading to God for justice, but is also making _himself_ accountable to God in the matter, so if there were any degree of culpability upon David, in his plea for rendering judgment from the Lord – he opens himself up to receive any correction or judgment in the matter as well:

"O LORD my God, _if_ I have done this: _If_ there is iniquity in my hands, _If_ I have repaid evil to him who was at peace with me, Or have plundered my enemy without cause,

Let the enemy pursue me and overtake me;
Yes, let him trample my life to the earth,
And lay my honor in the dust. *Selah*
(Psalms 7:3-5)

That is a gutsy approach to take before the Lord. But David loved and longed for truth… He knew that:

"Behold, You desire *truth* in the
inward parts, and in the hidden part
You will make me to know wisdom.'
(Psalms 51:6)

"Your Word have I have *hidden* in my heart,
that I might not sin against You."
(Psalms 119:11)

There was a situation in David's life where he was being accused by a person with significant charges. David's men offered to take the guy outside and deal with him, but David having the posture of heart he did said "No, wait, what if what he is saying is true?" David was willing to have his own heart searched by the Lord, by himself, as well as others…

"Search me, O God, and know my heart;
Try me, and know my anxieties;
And see if *there is any* wicked way in me,
And lead me in the way everlasting.
(Psalms 139:23-24)

That is the posture of heart necessary to present a *"shiggaion"* *song* of worshipful intercession and plea unto the Lord, asking for His judgment and deliverance (or vindication) in a storm brought on by the attack, deed or accusation of others.

It is brought forth in heavy and deep emotion and passion unto the Lord because of the intensity of the issue. That is why we sub-titled this chapter: *"Stirred Zeal – Mighty Justice!"*

You continue to see this posture of the heart of David in the next few verses of the Psalm 7 *"shiggaion"*:

"Arise, O LORD, in Your anger;
Lift Yourself up because of the rage of my enemies;
Rise up for me to the judgment You have commanded!
So the congregation of the peoples shall surround You;
For their sakes, therefore, return on high.
The LORD shall judge the peoples;
Judge me, O LORD, according to my righteousness,
And according to my integrity within me."
(Psalms 7:6-8)

David declares the outcome of evildoers in the land, and the sharp and swift judgments of God:

"Oh, let the wickedness of the wicked come to an end,
But establish the just;
For the righteous God tests the hearts and minds.
My defense *is* of God,
Who saves the upright in heart.
God *is* a just judge,
And God is angry with the wicked every day.
If he does not turn back,
He will sharpen His sword;
He bends His bow and makes it ready.
He also prepares for Himself instruments of death;
He makes His arrows into fiery shafts.

Behold, the wicked brings forth iniquity;
Yes, he conceives trouble and brings forth falsehood.

He made a pit and dug it out,
And has fallen into the ditch which he made.
His trouble shall return upon his own head,
And his violent dealing shall come down on his own
crown."
(Psalms 7:9-16)

The *"shiggaion"* is the perfect *song* to *sing* into <u>*your*</u> storm,
when you are being attacked or slandered by another.

Though you are lifting up this *song* unto the Lord – <u>*your*</u> very
song passes right through the *eye of the storm* and unto the
Lord Jesus Christ. But in your pursuit in becoming more and
more *Christ like,* you maintain an open heart to receive greater
truth and a willingness to learn things about yourself you
might have not seen before…

You let the Lord judge the situation but again… you have
become willing to accept any corrections or adjustments that
might come forth from any possible culpability on you part…
Your *"shigaion"* song should always close with:

"I will praise the LORD according to
His righteousness, and will *sing* praise
to the name of the LORD Most High."
(Psalms 7: 17)

A beautiful representation of the *"shiggaion" song* is found in
the Book of Habakkuk. In the 2nd chapter, the prophet
Habakkuk details the feeling of doom in the nation during the
years he was living and recording the words of this book.

Interestingly enough, as the prophet moves into the 3rd
chapter of the book, he records it as a *"shigionoth"* which is the
plural form of *"shiggaion"*.

This *"shigionoth"* is a perfect psalmic *song* to lift up to the Lord in the midst of <u>your</u> storm. It recounts the awesome and powerful works of God through history, as well as the righteous judgments of God. But it is also pleading with God from a standpoint of true faith – no matter what the circumstances are you find yourself – you have placed yourself at the mercy of God and His righteous judgments and justice. This is truly the pure *"shiggaion!"*

MATTHEW 6:12

THE ETERNAL SONG

"TOGETHER FOR ETERNITY"

Beloved, it is the prayer of the Author that this book will opened up some levels of new understanding concerning the power of *song* and the infinite possibilities therein.

We have looked into Eternity Past to see that song has its origins in Heaven long before the foundations of the earth was ever laid. We have looked down the corridor of Biblical history to see how crucial *song* has played a role in worship, intercession, warfare, breakthrough, prophecy, and intimacy with our Bridegroom King.

We have examined a preponderance (sufficient weight) of Scripture concerning the value, importance and place of *song* in the life of the believer, when encountering storms of every kind in <u>your</u> lives. Even to the point of understanding the importance of the storms themselves - that each have an important purpose in <u>your</u> spiritual development, regardless of their origin…

Oh that this book may provide some practical guidelines for both embracing and enduring the *coming* storms in your life, teaching each reader how they might **gain perspective** (from a heavenly and eternal posture… i.e. the mind of Christ), and then learn to **keep perspective** (focus) upon the Lord in perseverance and faith until the storms ends.

We must develop a process of rationale that instantly places every situation that comes into our lives into the light of eternity – and learn to appraise it from an **eternal perspective**.

"He has made everything beautiful in its time.
Also He has put **eternity in their hearts**, except
that no one can find out the work that God does
from beginning to end."
(Ecclesiastes 3:11)

Why would God put a portion of eternity in our hearts now, during this life? Why would the Lord even *reveal* to His creation that He has an eternal purpose for _us_ to fulfill in this lifetime? Why would the Lord tell us to **focus** on the eternal things and take of eyes _off_ of the temporal?

"While we do **not** look at the things which are seen,
but at the things which are not seen. For the things
which are seen are *temporary*, but the things which
are not seen are *eternal*."
(2 Corinthians 4:18)

From the truest sense of an **eternal perspective**, we have been chosen to become the ultimate companion, partner and spouse of God for all of eternity *future*. All of the trials, tribulations and tragedies and warfare we experience in this lifetime are just merely developmental preparations that help to empower us so that we may eventually step into the role as the Co-Regent Bride of Jesus to rule and reign with Him forever.

When we rightly divide the Word of Truth, we can see what the Bible says about these storms and what they will lead to:

"Therefore we do **not** lose heart. Even though our
outward man is perishing, yet the inward man is

being renewed day by day. For our light affliction, which is but for a moment, is **working for us** a far more exceeding and eternal weight of glory…"
(2 Corinthians 4:16-17)

That is true **eternal perspective**…

"And we know that _all things_ work together for **good** to those who love God, to those who are the called **according to His purpose**."
(Romans 8:28)

That does not mean that the hardships we face in this life are not without prolonged periods of pain and suffering from time to time. It is said that "_serenity_ is not the absence of conflict… but the Presence of God." The Lord assured us in His Word… "In this life… you shall have tribulation." But He also promised us:

"…If we suffer with Him, we shall also reign with Him."
(2 Timothy 2:12)

"Now if we are children, then we are heirs—heirs of God and _co-heirs_ with Christ, if indeed we _share_ in His sufferings **in order** that we may also _share_ in His Glory."
(Romans 8:17)

The Apostle Paul understood this. He learned to embrace all hardships in his life, knowing there was Divine (Eternal) purpose in each and every event, just look what he prayed:

"That I may _know_ Him and the power of His resurrection, and the _fellowship of His sufferings_, being conformed to His death, if, by any means,

I may attain to the resurrection from the dead."
(Philippians 3:10-11)

Paul had a *song* in his heart. An eternal song and an **eternal perspective**. Regardless of what kind of storms he encountered – he **kept perspective**…

"Not that I speak in regard to need, for I have
learned in whatever state I am, to be content:
I *know* how to be abased, and I know how to
abound. Everywhere and **in all things** I have
learned both to be full and to be hungry, both
to abound and to suffer need. I can do all things
through Christ who strengthens me."
(Philippians 4:11-13)

It doesn't mean there won't be many tears shed as we endure the dark nights (seasons) of testing, trial, tribulations and tragedies… But we must not lose our *song in the night*! Hold on! Hold on! Gain and then **keep eternal perspective**!

This is how important learning to keep perspective is when you encounter the category 5 hurricanes that will come into your life. Look at the life that Jesus modeled for us.

Jesus went through the severest of testing and trial – and in every situation emerged victoriously – because He learned to **kept eternal perspective** (focus).

"Looking unto Jesus, the Author and Finisher of
our faith, who **for the joy that was set before Him**
endured the cross, despising the shame, and has
sat down at the right hand of the throne of God."
(Hebrews 12:2)

Facing the most horrible scenario anybody could ever endure – a painful and agonizing death on a cross – Jesus was focused upon the will of His Father – and with **joy** *before Him* (that's what He saw) He victoriously overcame the greatest trial of all time! That's why He told us:

"These things I have spoken to you, that in Me
you may have peace. In the world you will have
tribulation; but **be of good cheer**, I have *overcome*
the world."
(John 16:33)

We too are *destined* to overcome. One day soon, we too will have a gloriously and triumphal entry into the gates of Heaven, the Eternal City. Though we have endured many storms throughout our lives:

"And I heard a loud voice from Heaven saying, "Behold,
the Tabernacle of God is with men, and He will dwell
with them, and they shall be His people. God Himself
will be with them and be their God. **And God will wipe
away every tear from their eyes**; there shall be **no more
death**, **nor sorrow**, **nor crying**. There shall be **no more
pain**, for the former things have passed away."
(Revelation 21:3-5)

Beloved, everything you have experienced and endure, as well as everything that lies ahead of you in this journey – isn't for nought… Your God is with you in every storm! He promised He would never leave you or forsake you! Do you know what else He has done?

"You number my wanderings;
Put my tears into Your bottle;
Are they not in Your book?

When I cry out to You,
Then my enemies will turn back;
This I know, because God is for me.
In God (I will praise His word),
In the LORD (I will praise His word),
In God I have put my trust;
I will not be afraid.
What can man do to me?
Vows made to You are binding upon me, O God;
I will render praises to You,
For You have delivered my soul from death.
Have You not kept my feet from falling,
That I may walk before God
In the light of the living?
(Psalms 56:8-13)

This is not where _your_ story _ends_... This is where _your_ story _begins_. It's _your_ fresh new Heavenly perspective – here and now.

May you walk with new confidence in Christ Jesus, encountering _every_ storm with **praise** (_singing_ into your storm) and with **purpose** (knowing _your_ storm is yet another Divine opportunity of preparation for your eternal role!